"I'm having a hard time keeping this just business..."

Matt leaned forward to kiss Chelly, lightly at first, his lips testing hers. Heat seared straight through her, settling in her core. Yes. She'd been wanting this from him for days. Since the first time she'd laid eyes on him in fact.

But it was wrong, really wrong.

Then his thumb stroked across her jaw so tenderly, she sighed and opened her mouth to his. Never in her life had a kiss done so much to her body. She thrummed from head to toe. And then she was lost in him.

When they parted, they were both breathing hard.

"That was—um, hot," she said. "Amazing...and hot."

She wasn't going to do this.

Then he pulled her back to him and she was lost again.

Dear Reader,

As I finish up the edits on this book, it's Veterans Day, a time of remembering those who have and continue to fight for our freedom. And the book comes out around July Fourth, which is a big holiday for us to celebrate those freedoms in America. It isn't lost on me that I can write my fun, sexy romances because of what these people have done for their country. I appreciate that freedom every day.

I try to keep these books light and fun, and I sometimes take a bit of literary license with my characters and their jobs. But I never ever lose sight of the men and women who put themselves in harm's way to protect us, whether they be Marines, Army, Navy, Air Force, Coast Guard, National Guard, Firemen or Police. There are those who always run toward the danger. They are a special breed. This book is dedicated to them.

Much love to you all!

Candace Havens

Candace Havens

Make Mine a Marine

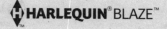

Recycling programs
for this product may
not exist in your area.

ISBN-13: 978-0-373-79904-6

Make Mine a Marine

Copyright © 2016 by Candace Havens

Printed in U.S.A.

Candace "Candy" Havens is a bestselling and award-winning author. She is a two-time RITA® Award, Write Touch Readers' Award and Holt Medallion finalist. She is also a winner of the Barbara Wilson Award. Candy is a nationally syndicated entertainment columnist for FYI Television. A veteran journalist, she has interviewed just about everyone in Hollywood. You can hear Candy weekly on New Country 96.3 KSCS in the Dallas–Fort Worth Area.

Books by Candace Havens

Harlequin Blaze

Take Me If You Dare
She Who Dares, Wins
Truth and Dare
Her Last Best Fling

Uniformly Hot!

Model Marine
Mission: Seduction
Her Sexy Marine Valentine

To get the inside scoop on Harlequin Blaze and its talented writers, be sure to check out BlazeAuthors.com.

All backlist available in ebook format.

Visit the Author Profile page at Harlequin.com for more titles.

1

CHELLY RICHARDSON ROLLED down the window of her beat-up truck and breathed in deep. And then she banged her head on the steering wheel three times.

This is not happening.

She tried the ignition again. Nothing. Her already awful twenty-four hours had hit a new low. After driving straight from Nashville to Corpus Christi, Texas, she was exhausted. When she couldn't get her new roommate to answer she'd taken a long nap at a truck stop located just outside of town. When she still couldn't get her friend to answer, Chelly picked up a paper and decided to hit some estate sales around town. That was what she did when she was nervous or upset. She went on a treasure hunt.

That was how she'd ended up in front of this plantation home, complete with a picturesque wraparound porch, where Old Joe—her truck—had decided to quit on her.

"I will not cry," she whispered. Even though she willed them away, tears threatened.

Why isn't Lila answering? That feeling Chelly some-times had when things weren't right niggled at her. When Chelly had called Lila on Wednesday, her friend had invited her to stay at her place for as long as she would need. Chelly was looking for a fresh start, away from Tennessee. Away from her ex, who'd become a little too attached to her. To being an almost-stalker. When he'd appeared at the diner where she was work-ing and created a scene, she'd given her notice, packed what few belongings she had and booked it out of town.

She didn't need that kind of drama. New life. New dreams.

Except now she couldn't get Lila to respond, and she didn't even have the address of her friend's house. Never one for planning much, this time her free-spirited ways had backfired.

I've been in worse jams.

Not really.

Oh, shut up. Anywhere was better than Nashville, where her ex had made her life miserable.

"Ma'am, are you okay?"

She glanced up from the steering wheel to find the hot guy from the estate sale looking in her passenger-side window. He was tall. At least six-three with a blond buzz cut that made her think he might be military. The bulging muscles under his T-shirt hadn't escaped her notice when she'd been looking through the high-end treasures at his sale. Treasures that she would have been more than happy to take off his hands if she'd had more than a hundred bucks to her name. His prices were way below market value, even for a quick sale.

She forced a smile.

"I'm fine," she said. "Thanks."

"Uh-huh. I saw you try the ignition but it didn't turn over. Didn't make a sound. Could be the battery, but may be the alternator."

Alternators were expensive; even a battery would take the last of her funds. Her throat clogged with emotion.

Oh, yay. This day just keeps getting better and better.

"If you pop the hood, I can take a look," he said.

Here was a guy, who quite obviously had better things to do, and he wanted to give her a hand? His kindness was her undoing. A lone tear escaped down her cheek and she brushed it away fast with the heel of her hand.

So dumb. I never cry.

"Hey, now. It'll be okay." His voice was deep and smooth, like a good whiskey. "Don't get upset. I'm pretty good with all things mechanical. I can help you, I promise."

She forced another smile. "Sorry. Just having a bad day. And Old Joe decided to remind me of Murphy's Law and has to be all stubborn because that's going to make a bad day even better." She sighed.

"I've been there," he said. "But it's gonna be all right. We'll get the truck running. Like I said, there isn't much I can't fix."

Maybe he wasn't military; he might be a mechanic. Or a superhero.

"Young man," an older woman interjected, waving at the hot guy. "How much do you want for the étagère?" She was pointing toward the Chinese Chippendale étagère that had left Chelly salivating.

Hot Guy took his aviators off, and she caught a glimpse of his beautiful dark green eyes. Wow. Total wow. He was gorgeous.

"Uh," he said. "How much do you want to pay?"

What? Did this guy not have a clue as to what he had here?

Before the woman could answer, Chelly was out of the truck and walking toward her. "It's five hundred, and that's final," she said.

The guy's eyebrow went up, though he didn't say anything.

"That's fair," the woman agreed. "Deal." She took five one-hundred-dollar bills from her purse and gave them to Chelly.

Then the woman turned back to Hot Guy. "Young man, can you please help me load the piece into my van?" She gestured at a pristine luxury SUV parked in front of the next house.

"Yes, ma'am. I'll be right there." To Chelly, he said, "No way that bookshelf is worth that much."

She smiled. "Not a bookshelf. It's an étagère and it's Chippendale. Retail it would go for around seventeen hundred."

He blew out a whistling breath. "And here I was going to sell it for twenty bucks, or whatever she offered."

Chelly almost choked. Hot Guy was absolutely clueless.

"Why did you have an estate sale if you don't know what you're doing?" She realized the words sounded harsh. "Sorry." She quickly backtracked. "I mean, there are companies who can do this for you."

He shrugged. "I assumed it wouldn't be this hard, and I didn't see why I should give a company twenty percent just to sell a bunch of junk."

She shook her head again. "You have no idea the quality of items you have here," she said. "This *junk* is worth thousands of dollars. It has lots of value. Even in the few larger pieces you have on the lawn, there's enough to buy a used car. In this neighborhood you're going to draw in a high-dollar clientele, and you need to take advantage of that. I don't live around here, but a neighborhood like this one is where antiques dealers go first. Most people have no idea what their stuff is worth."

He frowned. "You seem to know a lot about this."

"Everybody has their thing, mine is antiques. I love it all. It's kind of a hobby." A hobby she'd like to turn into a business someday.

"I have an idea," he said. "If you'll help me out, I'll fix your truck for free." He smiled, and she was glad she could hold on to the truck for support. The man was sexy from his blond hair to his superbly formed calf muscles and all points in between.

"I'm in over my head," he continued. "It's only nine a.m. If you'll stay until around three or so, I'll make sure your truck is ready by the time you want to go. And I'll pay for all the parts, and, as I said, labor is free."

Free parts. Hmm.

She asked, "And all I have to do is make sure all these sharks don't rob you?"

He smiled again, and her breath stuck in her lungs. "It's a fair trade. You just made me four hundred and eighty bucks more than I thought I would. The rest is gravy."

Well, there was nowhere else she needed to be at the moment, not that she could go anywhere without Old Joe. It was win-win.

Sticking out her hand, she shook his. "Deal." She tried to ignore the tingles that his warm fingers sent up her arm.

"I'm Matt, by the way."

"Chelly," she said. Then she realized she was still holding on to his hand. "Okay. I better get to work."

LIEUTENANT COLONEL MATT RYAN wiped his hands on the rag and then shut the hood of the old Ford F-150. After a quick run to the auto parts store, he had the vehicle going pretty good. He'd changed out the alternator and the oil, and bought her a new battery.

As he'd been working, he glanced over to find Chelly smiling and chatting with customers. Unlike him, she seemed to have an easy way with people. Her strawberry-blond hair was pulled back in a messy ponytail, and that blue blouse and denim shorts—man, she was about as pretty as they came. And she was smart about that junk. About five minutes after she'd started helping him out, she'd grabbed her phone from her truck. "I'm putting the details of your sale on one of the loops I'm on for antiques freaks." She took a few pictures and not long after that he had three times as many people on the property. It had been a steady stream ever since.

At lunch he'd stopped long enough to make sandwiches and tea for himself and Chelly. When he'd taken the lunch to her, she'd handed him a wad of cash. "I lost count, but you're close to three thousand. It's not safe to keep it out here. You should put it in the house somewhere." She frowned. "I mean, it seems like a lot of money, but you never know who might show up, especially in a neighborhood like this, where people know there's going to be good stuff."

Three thousand dollars before noon? It was insane. He'd thought he might get a couple hundred, maybe. The only reason he'd called it an estate sale was because the neighborhood association wouldn't allow him to refer to it as a garage sale. Chelly obviously knew what she was doing.

Occasionally, she'd asked him to carry some of the heavier items to people's vehicles.

He kept working on the truck and was surprised when he eventually looked up to find that there was hardly anything left on the lawn. She'd sold almost all of it.

He was a pretty self-sufficient guy. Rarely asked for help. But he'd needed it today. She was a wonder.

And he was most definitely a sucker for a beautiful woman. When he'd seen that tear fall onto Chelly's cheek earlier, he realized he'd do just about anything for her. He'd wondered who or what had made her cry. Wasn't his business. He had noticed the trash bags in the truck cab, and a couple of lamps and a table. She was either on her way out or on her way into town.

"You doing okay?" she asked.

He turned to find her approaching him with the cash box.

"You're all fixed up," he said, stuffing the dirty rag into the back pocket of his khakis.

"Really?" She gave him a sweet smile, and his lower region took notice.

"Yep."

She handed over the cash box. "You had a good haul today. There's at least thirty-five hundred in there, probably a little more."

What? He had no idea his parents' junk was worth that much. He opened up the cash box and took the money out. She deserved this. He already had the money she'd given to him earlier, and it was a lot more than he'd expected. "Here," he said, holding out the cash to her.

She waved him away. "What are you doing?"

"You deserve at least half," he said.

She stepped back. "No, we had a deal. You fix my truck, I sell your stuff."

"But you sold it for so much. You should get part of it. I don't feel right keeping all of this when you did the work. I had no idea what any of this stuff was."

She crossed her arms, still refusing to take the money. Odd, since he had a feeling she could use it. "Can I ask you something?" she said.

He nodded.

"Is this your house?" She pointed behind her.

"Yes."

"Are you getting divorced or something? Trying to get even with your ex by getting rid of all of her stuff for a fraction of what it's worth? I mean, I'm not judging, but I've been curious all day. You and what you're selling just don't seem to fit."

She had that last part right. "The furniture belonged to my parents who died last year in a car crash. I inherited the house and everything in it." Truth, he hadn't touched any of his parents' belongings in the house or the garage. What was sold today had been in a storage facility. His mom loved to collect furnishings. The items in storage he hadn't recognized, so it was easy to let go of them. But the rest, even though he needed to sell up, he couldn't bring himself to get rid of it, yet.

The loss tugged at his gut as it always did. After eight years in the Marines, he'd experienced a lot of loss. So many of his friends were gone, but his parents had always been his foundation. The tie that had kept him grounded. He could always go home.

And then they were killed. Gone in one night. And his world had come untethered.

"Oh." She put a hand on his arm and her warmth seeped into him. "I'm sorry. Figures I'd hit on a sore spot. My mouth always gets me into trouble."

"You didn't know. And it was a while ago. I'm only now starting to deal with all of this. Haven't been able to. I'm a Lieutenant Colonel in the Marine Corps."

"I don't blame you. And they had excellent taste, your parents. I apologize for prying."

"It's okay. Most of it was my mom's." It wasn't okay, actually, but he was a Marine, and he was pretty good at moving forward.

"So, thanks again for helping me with my truck. The few things that are left I've put in boxes for you. They're in the corner of the garage. All you have to do is fold up the tables. Do you have my keys? I should probably get going."

She was leaving. That bummed him out.

"Are you sure you won't take the cash?"

"Nope. I'm good, but thanks. This was fun for me."

"Your idea of fun and mine are completely different," he said.

They shared a look and he realized how his words could be misconstrued.

"Keys are in the ignition. Be safe." He felt like he wanted to hug her, but she was a stranger. That would be weird. Even weirder was the fact that he wasn't the hugging type.

While he knew a lot about sadness, Chelly seemed to embody it. Even when she smiled it didn't quite reach her eyes. A woman so beautiful shouldn't have those kinds of worries. No person should have the burden she seemed to be carrying.

He waved goodbye and then headed over to collapse the tables. He was about to shut the garage door when he noticed she was still sitting in her truck.

Was she having car trouble again? He'd checked everything out, and had even driven the truck around the block to make sure it was okay. As he drew closer, he saw that she was staring at her phone as if it were an alien. Her teeth worried her bottom lip.

"What's wrong?" he asked as he walked up to the driver's side.

She jumped.

"Sorry, didn't mean to scare you. You okay?"

She shook her head. "I, uh. My friend texted me. She got married…in Vegas." She sounded desolate.

"And that's bad?"

"No. I'm happy for her." She worried that bottom lip again. He had an urge to run his thumb across it.

What is wrong with me? The woman was having a difficult day. The last thing she needed was being ogled by him. "I'm not the best judge of emotions, but I'm pretty sure that's not a happy face." He pointed to her.

That made her smile, slightly. "Really, I am happy for her. She's loved this guy for a long time. He surprised her with a trip to Vegas last night. They were married at a drive-through chapel."

"That might not be the most romantic place to get married, but if you're happy for her, what's the problem?"

She rubbed the bridge of her nose with her thumb and forefinger. He had an urge to brush her hair from her cheek and tell her everything was going to be okay, even though he had no idea what was going on.

"I drove here from Nashville to be her roommate. I was supposed to move in today."

Realization dawned.

The roommate had filled the position with a new husband.

"So you're—"

"Homeless."

2

CHELLY TRIED TO keep a positive attitude through the downs of life, but the last month had about done her in. Between the stalker ex and everything she'd gone through emotionally and financially, she was on the slow train to oblivion. Those dark places she tried not to dwell in were closing in on her.

"That's rough." The Marine leaned in her window. He gave her a look of pity. She hated that.

"I've been through worse. I'll be fine." And she would. It wasn't as if she hadn't been in bad situations before now. There was that time in Turkey when she'd nearly been thrown in jail, and in Mumbai when she had that bug that laid her up for three days in some stranger's house.

She sat up a little straighter and took a deep breath.

He nodded. "Strong. That's a good character trait. But you look like you could use a break, and to be honest, I'd like to get away from the house for a bit. Do you have a swimsuit in that luggage of yours?" He nodded at the trash bags, aka all her worldly belongings in the back of her truck.

Where was he going with this?

Her thoughts must have shown on her face because he chuckled. "I'm not sure what you're imagining, but I was going to grab some dinner and head out to my favorite place to clear my head. You're welcome to join me, unless you have better plans?"

He had her there. "Are you a serial killer?"

He frowned. "No. Uh, I'm not."

Shoot. She'd done it again. "Are you sure you want to hang out with me? I have a tendency to say the wrong thing *all* the time."

"Well," he said, a slow smile gracing his mouth, "I think I can handle it for the next few hours. Why don't you pull around back and we can park your truck in one of the garages. That way your stuff will be safe. Get what you need and I'll meet you there. Go down the street and turn into the alley."

She should tell him no and move on, but he was right. She had nowhere else to go, and she did need a break. Dinner with Hot Guy was not the worst option. "Okay."

His smile actually made her heart beat a little faster. *No! No more men.*

A few minutes later, she had her change of clothes, a bikini and her flip-flops and was waiting by the two-story garage. The building was almost as long as the house, and it looked like there was an apartment on top. His parents must have had a great deal of money. This place was at least two and half acres in the middle of one of the nicest neighborhoods in town.

At least from what she'd seen so far.

When Lila had said she could move in, Chelly had looked up Corpus Christi and saw there was a beach. That was all she cared about, being near the water. She'd been tired of being landlocked in Nashville. Just one more reason to move.

The grime from having driven for so long was now starting to get to her. She couldn't wait to hit the waves.

The garage door opened and she saw Matt standing there in board shorts and a clean white tank shirt. Those arm muscles were a powerful aphrodisiac.

Hey, that's the last thing you need! No guys—it was the number-one rule she'd made in the first hour of her road trip. Ever. Well, at least not until she had her business in a good place and her life straightened out.

"You can park in this bay, but let me move my bike first." He rolled out a black motorcycle. It was big and powerful-looking, just like him. A sexy Marine on a motorcycle.

No! Just say no.

She gave him a quick grin as she pulled into the garage. That was when she realized what he meant about his mother's collection. There was a new Ford truck in the next bay, but the rest of the garage was filled with antiques.

"Heaven," she whispered.

He laughed as he opened her door to help her out. "Maybe to you. To me, it's nothing but a headache. I have no idea what's expensive or not. I mean, I can tell from some of the wood—walnut and maple—that it's worth something, but I don't know what year anything was made or the value of it."

From where she stood, she saw a wardrobe from the eighteen hundreds and, if she wasn't mistaken, the buffet was from the same period. "Do me a favor, when you decide to sell all of this, call me first? This is a gold mine. These things should be in an air-conditioned space. The heat and moisture will play havoc with the wood."

He winced. "I collected it all in here so I could sort through it. I didn't know."

"How long ago was that?"

"About a month," he told her.

Not too bad. "Should be fine for now. But you need to make sure none of it gets wet or it'll warp. It's warm and humid, but if it the temperature goes higher, you might want to think about moving the stuff back indoors, until you sell it. I can help you, though, at least, figure out what you should get for the really good pieces. You won't get retail prices, but there are five or six premium items in here."

He made a face and grunted. "You serious?"

"Oh, yeah."

"Huh. Okay. I'll have to take you up on that because I've got a lot of renovations to do." He pointed at the bike. "We better get on the road if we're going to be at my favorite spot in time."

She wondered in time for what, but she figured he wanted to surprise her. After closing the garage door from a keypad, he passed her a helmet. She pulled it over her curls and then he helped strap it around her chin.

He climbed on the bike.

She eyed him warily. Not that she minded putting her arms around the hunk, but they had just met.

"I hope this is okay. It's easier to use the bike rather than the truck to get where we're going."

She happened to like bikes and she didn't want to insult the guy who had done her a favor and fixed her truck. "Works for me."

He sat down on the massive seat. The sign on the side of the dark blue bike said Harley. She had some regulars at the diner where she'd worked who rode them. The chrome bike was a piece of art. It was customized with some slogans, Semper Fi she recognized, and a symbol she wanted to look up later.

"You can sit back here," he said, patting the seat behind his. "Be careful of your calves with the exhaust pipe. Keep your feet up on the foot pads and you should be good."

She did as she'd been told, but considered if her sneakers would have been a better choice, instead of the flip-flops. Though he was wearing flip-flops, so she wasn't worried. What she didn't know was where to put her hands. "You can wrap your arms around my chest or hold on to my shoulders. I recommend the chest since it'll be easier where we're going."

He started the bike and the monster rumbled between her thighs. She wrapped her arms around his hard chest. He must work out every day, she thought.

Her fingers itched to slide down and feel the rigid abs she knew were only a few inches below.

She was concentrating so hard on him that it was a good five minutes before she realized Matt had already driven them to the beach. The salty smell bit into her senses. She loved the water.

He steered into a burger joint and turned off the bike. "I'll be right back, I'm going to grab us some dinner. Anything you don't like?"

She shook her head, still trying to deal with the throbbing between her legs.

"I won't be long." Five minutes later he came out with armfulls of food, sodas and bottles of water. He stowed them in one of the side compartments of the bike.

"I could have helped you," she said as he climbed back onto the motorcycle.

"No problem. I'm pretty hungry so I got a little of everything. We're heading over there." He lifted his chin toward the nearby hill and then put the bike into gear.

They rode right out onto the beach. It was slightly elevated and marked private. He stopped the bike and she climbed off.

"Is it okay for us to be here?" she asked.

He pulled a blanket out of the other side compartment and handed it to her. "It's owned by some friends of mine. They let me use it whenever I want. Their place is up there." He pointed up the hill again to a stunning beach house. "They're gone this weekend, or there would probably be a whole crew of people running around. It's the go-to spot for a lot of us on the base, especially on the weekends. Put the blanket by the fire pit. I'll bring the food and meet you down there."

The sun was just above the horizon, and the reflection was unforgettable on the blue water and white sand. The waves were calling to her. "Do you mind if I swim before we eat?"

"That was the plan," he said as he stripped of his tank and took off his flip-flops.

Oh. My. Those abs. Seriously. She had to stop herself from gasping. They made men well in Texas. Very well.

After he'd gone into the ocean, she took off her top and shorts and adjusted her bikini, eager to cool her too-heated body. The water was actually warm. Still, it was wet and it felt good to ease the tension from her body. She followed Matt out to a sandbar.

"This is my favorite place to watch the sunset," he said. She could see why. The water was shimmering, as if topped with sparkling diamonds.

"Are those starfish?" she asked.

"Yes. Last winter there was a cold spell and a lot of them washed up on the beach. Volunteers helped get them back out to sea. Marine biologists say their efforts helped save more than half the local population."

"I've always been fascinated by starfish and sea-horses," she said, and she bent down to get a better look.

He cleared his throat. "We have those, as well, though you probably have to snorkel in one of the coves to see them. We also have a great aquarium in town."

"Cool. I'll have to check it out." It felt a bit strange, hanging out with this man she didn't know, yet she was more relaxed than she'd been in months. Maybe it was the water, or the pure exhaustion of the day.

Then, from the corner of her eye, she spotted something. She reached out to touch Matt's arm. "Fin," she said quietly as she backed away and tried to step off the sandbar for the shore.

He took her hand tightly. "Not what you think," he whispered into her ear. "Watch." Suddenly, a dolphin leaped through the air, splashing them on the way down.

Chelly let out a strangled laugh. "That totally scared me." The dolphin leaped again and then there was another one. It was almost as if they were playing a game.

He laughed, too. "They come around this time to play and eat. You do have to watch for sharks, though, but that's usually later in the summer. We have bull and tiger sharks that can sometimes be aggressive. But the dolphins are here pretty much year round, unless the water cools too much and then they swim south to Mexico."

Sharks were on her list of things she never wanted to meet, but she trusted Matt to keep her safe. As the sun set, shivers traveled up her arms. He must have noticed because he glanced down to where he held her hand and let go. "You ready to eat?"

"Sure."

Back on the beach he got a couple of towels from where the blanket had been stored on his bike and he handed her one. They ate their burgers and fries as the sun went down.

But it was far from dark. The moon was a bright globe in the night sky.

"This has been one of the best days I've had in a while," she murmured. "Sitting here, watching the waves, I can almost forget all the crazy."

"It's the best place to just be. Sometimes I have trouble with that," he said. "Sitting and being still. I prefer to stay busy. But this is the one spot where it's easy for me to catch my breath."

She had a feeling there was more to that story. What military men and women went through tore at her heart. But, like her, they didn't appreciate pity, either.

"I have that same problem. Always on the go. I always have too many irons in the fire, but I kind of like it that way. However, I could do without the recent drama."

Shoot. That just slipped out.

He leaned back on his arms and glanced over at her. "If it helps, you can talk about it. I'd assumed you're on the run from something or someone."

She grinned. "So you think I might be a criminal, but you're hanging out with me, anyway?"

He cocked an eyebrow. "You're a really good salesperson, so I'm not complaining. Hey, the fact is you made me thousands of dollars today and gave me every cent. You refused the cash even though you deserved it for all the hard work you did."

She took a deep breath. "I'm not on the run from any criminal activities. And I'm not a con man or—con person—or…whatever—" She gave an unladylike snort. "Sorry. That's just funny to me. The sales thing, well, that's a passion for old stuff, really. I mentioned it's my thing."

"You drove all night from Nashville, why the rush?"

I had to get the heck out of Dodge.

When she didn't answer right away, he said, "You don't have to tell me."

"My ex," she said. Why not say it? This guy had been nothing but kind to her, and she'd probably never see him again. "We broke up a while ago, but he didn't seem to get the memo. When he threw a tantrum at the diner where I was working, I realized it probably wasn't safe for me to be there."

Matt quickly sat up. "Did he hurt you?" He very nearly growled the words.

"No. He scared me...bad. Frightened me, actually. I wanted nothing to do with him after that. And when I wouldn't accept his apology... It's complicated."

"What happened?"

"He came to the diner again, caused a big scene in front of everyone. I'd been full-time there so a lot of the customers knew me. It was creepy, embarrassing. I took off and never looked back."

She shifted to her side. Her story sounded like an episode from one of those crime shows on TV. How had her life slipped so far out of control? "That was the second time it had happened, and my boss said if it happened a third time, he was calling the cops. I couldn't blame him. I was thinking the same thing."

"I hate jerks who harass women. They should be locked up."

Yup. She really liked this guy.

"It's okay, Marine. I told you, I got out of that situation."

"True. Please, finish your story."

"We'd only been dating a few months and he seemed really great and attentive. But when he drank, I wasn't so sure about his emotional stability. And *that guy*, I wanted nothing to do with him. That's why I booked it. It was just easier. And Nashville was so not the right place for me. I mean, it's a great town and all, just not my style."

He'd probably think she was a runner and he wouldn't be wrong. She hated confrontation, and when things got too tough she did have a habit of walking away. Her parents would be the first to sing hallelujah to that. She'd never stuck with anything for very long and as such was a constant disappointment to them.

But then, they weren't exactly aces in her book, either. She hadn't run so much as been pushed out of their house.

"You shouldn't have had to leave town. Your home. That guy should be taught a lesson." Matt sounded like he might want to teach that lesson. Did Matt have a violent streak? So far, all indications were he was about as kind as they came.

He was taking her side in all this, that's it, which was what friends did. And she could definitely use one of those right now.

"I'll be honest, it wasn't much of a home. I'd only been there for a year. I've been traveling a lot. Roots haven't been important to me for a long time. That's why I was working at the diner. Easiest job to find in that area."

He shook his head. "Wow. That still stinks. I'm sorry."

She laughed. It was kind of absurd—the last year. It was like the universe was trying to show her something and she wasn't seeing it. "I've developed a few trust issues, it's true."

"Who wouldn't?"

Chelly tried not to hold on to anger and disappointment. They were useless emotions, but sometimes it was hard.

He leaned back again. "I'm sorry you've had such a bad time. I've only known you a day, but you seem pretty nice. And no one deserves to be treated like that."

No pity, just kindness. She appreciated that.

"Thanks. What doesn't kill you makes you stronger, right?" And then she slapped a hand across her mouth. Why did she keep saying such dumb things? "Sorry."

He frowned. "For what?"

"I keep saying silly things like that around you. I'm sure you've had to deal with really serious things— way tougher than anything I might have been through. I mean, nothing compares to what you guys have to endure when you're deployed. I've heard stories from some of the veterans at the diner. I'm always saying the wrong thing at the wrong time—"

"You don't need to be careful with me," he said. "My parents walked on eggshells whenever I came home, and it drove me crazy. Mom tried to put whale sounds in my room to keep me calm. Well, I kind of liked the whales. But I do what I do because I like the idea of making a difference. Being a Marine does that for me. And I've had it easier than most.

"Mom and Dad always did things their own way. We were never what you'd call normal. Of course, I'd give anything to have them around now to drive me nuts. Just know, with me, you can say whatever you want. I don't ever think about comparing my life with anyone's. Everybody goes through tough times. Sounds like you've had your fair share."

Until I met you today. "I had a Sunday school teacher once who said that sometimes we put obstacles in our path, and sometimes they are put there to guide us down the right path. I never really understood that until this year. I don't know where my path is going, but Nashville was definitely a wrong turn for me. I learned a lot of lessons there, none of which I intend to repeat."

"I don't usually believe in all those universe theories, but something good led you to my estate sale today, so I'm grateful."

Shoot. She was grateful for the change of subject. "That's sweet. I was glad to help."

"Can I ask you something?" He shifted from where he'd been sitting.

"Sure. You know the majority of my darkest secrets." At least the most recent ones.

"Why don't you do this—the antiques thing—for a living?"

She glanced away from him and stared out at the water. Her dream had been so close to her heart for so long. Each time she thought she might be a step closer, something else happened.

"Hey," he said, touching her shoulder lightly, and she looked at him. "No judgments. I promise."

He stared at her intently. She could get so lost in those eyes.

Friend. Keep him in the friend zone.

"Okay, but don't say I didn't warn you."

3

Matt liked listening to Chelly talk about her idea for a junk repurposing business. She was so passionate about it, and her hands and mouth were going a hundred miles an hour. The towel slipped off her shoulder and exposed her bikini top. Thankfully, those dolphins showed up when they did earlier, or she would have seen his erection. When she'd bent over to touch the starfish, he couldn't look away from her perfect butt. She was curvy in all the right places and seemed so comfortable with her body. He liked a woman who was confident.

Chelly cleared her throat. "I'm boring you. Sorry."

"Not at all. So you take the old furniture, like my mom has in the garage, and turn it around and sell it for a profit?"

"Your mom's furniture, at least what I saw of it, you would never touch. Painting or staining those things can ruin the value of the piece. But like that one desk we sold today—the school desk? It's something that I could paint or do a fun pattern on or switch it into something else and it would bring in more money than the original would."

"And you want to sell online?" He was getting the gist and trying to think of a way to give her a hand. That was something his mom had instilled in him. When you could do something nice for someone, you did it.

"To start with, yes. Someday I'd love to also have a storefront. And my ultimate goal is to build up my cash reserves so I can buy a retail warehouse. I never want to be in debt, so I'd save up first. I'm thinking solar panels for the roof to get off the grid as much as possible and save on costs and spare the earth. I know it's probably a long way off, but a girl's gotta dream. I like being self-sustainable."

"I get it," he said. And he did. An idea began to form in his mind. "So what if...and it's okay for you to say no."

She bit her lip. He noticed she did that when she was worried. "What did you have in mind?"

"We might be able to help each other out and in the process get your business started."

Her eyes widenened. She asked, "How?"

"It's clear that I have no clue what to do with all of my parents' belongings. Some of those furnishings I want to save for my place, which I'm going to start building, but the rest I need to sell. Maybe you could assist me with that. I could give you a percentage and then anything that you might be able to repurpose, you could have for your business. I'd only be taking those items to the dump or giving them to charity, anyway."

"You don't have to do that. I'd help you for free," she

said. Still, she wouldn't look at him. He'd pay big bucks to know what she was thinking just then.

"Nope. I need an expert and this only works if I feel it's fair. You made me over six thousand today. I realize I keep saying that, but it's so much more than I ever imagined. You get that I have no experience at this, and you'd be protecting me, as well. Making sure I get decent prices. You could build up an inventory. I bet that's important. My mom used to have a store, which is why we have all this crap in the first place."

"She had an antiques store? Now it makes sense. Everything was from different time periods and styles, and I couldn't figure out how she would fit all of that in one house." She smiled then, and her gaze met his. "It's not crap, by the way. She had exquisite taste."

"See? That's why I need you." He did.

"Do you do this with everyone you meet? Try to fix them? Sort out their lives? Is that, like, your thing?"

He crossed his legs and sat up. "What do you mean?"

"Saving damsels in distress. You're a Marine. You're probably wired to rescue people."

Maybe he was, but it started a long time before the Marines. "You don't really seem the type that needs to be rescued. I was thinking more of you being the one to save me, which is why it's okay if you say no. There won't be any hard feelings on my part."

She shook her head. "You're kind of a wonder, Matt. I'm not sure what to think."

Given what she'd been through, she probably was a little shy about trusting anyone. He had the same problem, and he wasn't quite sure why he was inviting her into his life. Over the past few months he'd done little except focus on work and make lists about what he wanted in his new house. Thinking of building it was the only light he had at the end of the tunnel.

He'd been forcing himself to go out with his friends, but more than anything he wanted to be on his own. To live peacefully. Get everything organized so he could move forward. He liked things ordered.

He had a feeling chaos followed Chelly, but there was something special about her. Something that called to him. The last few hours on the beach had been some of the most peaceful he'd experienced.

"You said you wanted to sell your family home. Can I ask why?"

That caught him off guard. "I have some river property not far from here, where I'd like to build a place. With the sale of Mom and Dad's house I can afford it. I'm not much of a suburb kind of guy. I like my privacy. I've been meeting with an architect the last few weeks, but I really have to get my parents' home and furnishings settled first."

She seemed to consider this. "You mentioned you wanted to save some of their possessions for your place. What kind of a place? A cabin?"

"Nah. Can I show you?" He got out his phone, opened a real estate app and presented her with a photo of the iconic Texas river house he wanted. "It's called a Texas T. Family room and kitchen in the center with hallways off to other rooms. And I want limestone floors and whatever else makes it fit into the landscape naturally."

She flipped through the pictures. "Wow. This is incredible."

He wasn't sure why it pleased him that she liked it so much, but it did. "Here, I'll show you the view from where I'm hoping the family room will be." He took the phone and opened a new file of photos and handed it back to her.

She blinked. "*That's* your view? Looking right out on the river? It's totally incredible. And those cliffs. It looks like something on a postcard."

That's what he'd been thinking. When he was a kid he used to play in the woods around there while his dad and uncle fished in the river. Where the house sat was up on a rise, but there were a hundred acres, most of that on the riverfront. He'd been offered top dollar for it, but it was one of the most quiet, peaceful places on earth, and no way was he giving it up.

"You said you picked out an architect? Do you have a designer?" Her words came quickly now, her excitement was contagious.

He smiled.

"I hadn't thought about a designer," he answered. "One of my friends, Brody, is marrying a designer. She looked over the plans for me and told me how to— what did she say?—oh, to maximize the view. I guess I figured I could just ask her. Though, Brody says she's busier than ever these days."

"Or I could do that. Help you, I mean." She worried her bottom lip. "Sorry, it's just when I saw what you wanted, and where it's going to be, I had all these visions in my head. Like you should use river rock for the fireplace. And I'd do limestone in the kitchen, but you have to make sure it's sealed really good. You might think about using bamboo flooring for the rest, though. It'll be a little warmer in the winter and it wears really well. If you're running around barefoot all the time, the limestone might be a bit rough on your feet. And the wood will give the place a homier feel."

He'd never thought of that. He did like wood flooring.

"Or not," she continued just as quickly. "Like I said, I tend to jump into things pretty fast. That's why I wasn't so sure about your offer with the business. It's been my experience, especially lately, that if it sounds too good to be true, it probably is. Whether that be business or men."

He didn't blame her. "I get that. So in the spirit of being honest, before we get started you should maybe know that I like things done a certain way, and it's hard for me to let go of that."

"I'm kind of the opposite. If we're going to do this, you'll have to trust me to handle the details."

A long moment passed before he said, "I guess it won't hurt to try. I'd be willing to draw up a contract for you to organize, sell and repurpose my parents' stuff. How do you feel about a sixty-forty split?"

"If I'm getting the forty, I can roll with that."

He'd been thinking the split should go the other way, since she'd be doing a hundred percent of the work. "Okay, if that's what you want. But it would be fairer if you took the bigger—"

"I take forty," she interrupted. "I'd be happier with thirty. Forty seems really high."

"Nope. That's where I draw the line. I'd feel like I was taking advantage of you."

She shrugged. "I'm guessing this is how nice people do business."

They both laughed.

"For help with the river house, come up with a flat fee to charge me for your design ideas and dealing with the architect. I know what I like, but getting that across to folks—I'm not always the best communicator."

She snorted and then clapped a hand over her mouth. He kind of loved that she did that. "That's so not true. You're easy to talk to. Maybe it's the other people who are doing the bad listening." She grinned.

"You might be right. So, good. Oh, and there's one more thing."

The grin disappeared.

"I know how to build a website. I did one for my mom's business several years ago." His friends called him a geek, but he was the go-to guy when computers, phones or anything else broke. He'd always liked tinkering with things, machines in general. He was a pilot, but he was also a fully vetted helicopter mechanic.

"Now you're scaring me," she said. And he could see that he really did. "You're a little too perfect. Definitely an ax murderer, right?"

He rolled his eyes. "I'm far from perfect. Just ask anyone who knows me." On the base he'd been reamed for not playing well with others. But he just liked to keep to himself. Though, he really had been trying to do better. The CO's team-building events had forced it on him, but they'd also helped him to not be a complete loner, which was probably a plus.

"Honestly, ax murderer or not, I can't wait to get started." Then her face fell again.

"What?"

"Nothing. So, I can start tomorrow?"

"I gotta be on base by nine, but as long as you're at my parents' early, I can let you in. Before we head back there now, we can stop and get whatever you might need."

That's when it hit him. He'd helped her with the job situation—but she had nowhere to live.

And that was one line he wasn't ready to cross.

4

CHELLY'S LIFE HAD done a one-eighty into awesome, but she wasn't sure she could trust the feeling. Everything had been so rotten lately that she spent most of her time waiting for the other shoe to drop. But during her long drive from Tennessee, she'd promised herself that she'd start living in the moment again. Like she used to when she left college. Life had been better then, albeit a little on the gypsy side. She'd traveled the world and found odd jobs to fund the journey. Living in the here and now and taking advantage of opportunities had worked for her back then.

And maybe it would again. Mr. Marine had offered her an amazing opportunity. One that she would be silly to turn down. And it didn't come with strings, which was beyond unusual. Matt was off gathering firewood for the pit, in order to roast the magical bag of marshmallows he'd had hidden in that Harley of his.

This guy. Well, she wasn't sure what to think. It was so strange that all of this had happened. He was super-nice, although she had a feeling he didn't think of himself as such. But he'd already been so generous. Fixing her truck and taking her to the beach, offering to help her out.

He was right about his needing her expertise. Estate sale folks and resale shops would charge him huge fees. For the river house, she was determined he'd accept her modest one. She was already stoked about the ideas she had for the place.

She hadn't lied. His pictures had sent her mind whirling.

"Here's your stick," he said.

She glanced up, confused. "I soaked it in the sea a bit so it won't burn. Might make the marshmallows taste a little salty."

She laughed. Right. "People pay a lot of money for sea salt marshmallows and sea salt caramel ones, too."

His eyebrows drew together. "That's a thing?"

"Sure."

He held out a hand to her and she stood up. "Who knew we were making gourmet marshmallows in the fire pit?"

"Since we're being honest with each other, I should admit that I can pretty much eat my weight in marshmallows. Easily a whole bag in one sitting. So, fair warning."

"Oh, it's so on," he said. And then proceeded to put four marshmallows on his stick. She promptly put five on hers.

Laughing, she said, "Thanks. Today showed me that there are still good people in the world. I really needed to be reminded of that."

"Hey, I feel the same. I guess it's lucky that you like junk and that your truck conked out in front of my house. Uh, maybe that's not so great, but at least you weren't out on the highway or stuck in the middle of nowhere. There's a lot of middle of nowheres between here and Nashville."

"I know, right? Old Joe actually did me a favor. Maybe things are looking up."

They were, but she still didn't trust the feeling.

Live in the moment.

"So do you have a place to stay for the night?"

And there was the other shoe dropping. Sigh. Did he expect favors? He didn't seem the type. No, she didn't have a place, but she definitely wasn't staying with him.

He lifted his marshmallows from the fire and blew on them. "That didn't come out how I meant it to, Chelly. I wasn't hitting on you. Just so you know. Honest."

"I'm good."

His eyebrow shot up. "You said your friend was out of town."

"Yep. But I'm good," she repeated. She had no idea what she was doing for shelter and she didn't have much cash. Her plan was to head back out to one of the truck stops and sleep there. "I like camping and there are plenty of good places around here."

"All right. You should know, though, that there are several guest rooms in my parents' house. Or there's the apartment over the garage. But none of those rooms have been touched in more than a year. And the apartment is filled with furnishings. There's the pool house, but it's basically a bed, desk and shower. I could give you some money for a hotel? A cash advance against what you make with my mom's furniture? Might be more comfortable for both of us, and there are some decent hotels close by."

He didn't even want her staying with him. For some reason that struck her as being funny and she started laughing. Why would he? She was a mess. And he was a guy who liked order. He wasn't kidding about that. From the way he'd organized their dinner on the blanket, to his need to clean up afterward before they moved on to dessert. "I appreciate the kindness, but I promise, I have it covered."

She'd noticed showers attached to the campgrounds down the coast. Maybe she'd just hole up there for a bit.

The look he gave her was full of disbelief, but he didn't say anything else. They ate their marshmallows in silence.

An hour later they were back at his parents' place. She backed her truck out of the garage, sort of sad to end the day.

In fact, part of her was worried that if she left, he'd change his mind when she returned tomorrow morning.

Her phone rang; it was the ex. She looked away. With her first bit of cash she was going to switch accounts and get a different number. The jerk had given her the phone for her birthday. It had been nice at the time. Now, not so much.

Then it dawned on her. What if he could track her GPS? Is that how he'd found out where she was all the time? He'd shown up at the grocery store, the nail salon, the...

"Shoot." She turned the phone off.

"What's wrong?"

She jumped. Matt was standing at her truck window, but he backed off when he saw she was scared.

Her hand went to her chest. "Sorry. It's dawned on me that my ex could be tracking my phone. He just called. I don't suppose you have a tub of water or a very deep pool you could throw this phone in? You mentioned a pool house. I'm praying he hasn't tracked me down yet."

"Follow me," he said. And then he held his hand out for the phone.

"Wait." She turned the phone back on and sent a text.

I'm really gone. You need to stop calling. Truck broke, so I'm taking a bus to Mexico. Phone won't work there. Adios forever.

She hit Send, and as soon as it showed he'd read it, she clicked off the phone again and handed it to Matt.

"This way." She trailed after him through the garage and out to the most glorious backyard she'd ever seen. It was a Garden of Eden with a huge pool and a large patio that had a mix of teak and black iron lawn furniture. Along the fence line there were magnolia trees and freesias mixed with jasmine. The smell alone was magical, but there were twinkling lights, as well. When she was a kid, she couldn't have imagined a better land for fairies. Oh, who was she kidding? She couldn't imagine a better place now.

Except for New Zealand. Oh, how she missed that country.

"Did your parents entertain a lot?" she asked, before she realized that that might be another painful memory.

"All the time. Any excuse for a party. Holidays were my mom's favorite, but they had friends over a lot."

"I can imagine. This place is terrific. I'd never want to leave."

"I used to complain about it when I was kid because I was always on pool-cleaning duty, and I was also the official toilet scrubber."

She couldn't help the giggle that escaped. "Yeah, I bet that would get old very fast."

He sighed dramatically, but then gave her a wide, warm smile. "You have no idea. I also had to dust a lot of my mom's collectables. That was the worst. I never broke anything. Still, she wouldn't have cared if I did. She was easygoing. But my dad on the other hand would have grounded my butt for a month if I'd broken something of hers."

Even though he complained, he didn't sound like it really bothered him. These were fond memories.

She didn't have many of those with her parents. Maybe, when she was younger, but that was a long time ago.

"So do you want to do the honors?"

He held out the phone and she took it. "That hot tub looks like a good start," she said. And then she bent down and dropped it in. It was freeing—losing this last bit of her old life. Sure, she might need some of those numbers again, but she'd cross that bridge when she came to it—namely when she was able to get a new phone.

Shoot. She forgot about Lila's number. Now she had

no way of getting in touch with her. Wasn't meant to be? What kind of friend invited you to come live with her and then didn't give you the address or leave you a key when she went off to get married?

She had to work on meeting better people.

After leaving her cell in the water for several minutes, she walked across to the pool and dropped the phone on the first step. "Do you have a water hose?"

He chuckled. "Behind the gardenias, over there in the corner." She followed his directions and saw the faucet and hose attached. She only took a few seconds to drown the cell, not wanting to waste too much water.

"Are you sure you don't want to hit it with a sledge-hammer?"

She considered it. "No, too messy. Though I might run over it with the truck a few times just to make sure."

"We have some tanks at the base," he joked.

"Ha, that's good. Thank you for everything. This turned out to be a great day."

"Yeah, for me, too. Can I show you one more thing before you go?"

She lifted her shoulders. "Sure."

He led her around the lawn to the pool house. It was cute, with the same kind of antebellum architecture that was on the front of the main house. It even had black shutters. She'd expected it to be bare, except for the basics he'd said would be there, but when he opened the doors and switched on the light, she nearly passed out from what was before her.

"This is so different than what I expected," she said as she took in the shabby-chic furniture. There was a

French daybed that had been made into a little reading nook. On the other side of the room, an office had been set up with a beautiful white desk—very French. Everything was blue and white, except for the curtains, which were a gray-and-white toile.

"She was in the process of redoing the whole house. But she redid her office first. After she sold the shop, she continued to deal online, so she'd needed a dedicated space away from Dad. He gets—I mean, he got kind of loud when he was watching sports, and it drove her nuts."

"Nothing in here is like what she has out in the garage," she said. All the other items were very formal, very expensive; all of this was also chic, but in a more whimsical way.

"True. All that junk is pretty stuffy. I'll show you tomorrow in more detail. Anyway, I was thinking, there's air-conditioning and a shower and a bed. And you could use it for tonight. There's even a good lock on the door, so you'd be safe."

From him? As if she was worried about that now.

"Matt, you're sweet. But I told you—"

"You're not a damsel in distress. I know. But I am a worrier. The campgrounds are probably fine, but your ex might have some idea where you are and that bothers me. You said he wasn't dangerous, but if he's following your every move… I'd feel better if you were secure. Besides, you can use this as your office until you find more permanent digs. My mom would love that another antiques lover is using her space.

"And, um. Well…"

Was she really going to say no to staying in a palace fit for a princess? She couldn't have dreamed of a more perfect space for herself. "Matt, what is it?"

"It's probably asking a lot, given you've already agreed to handle the contents of my parents' house and my new place. But the real estate agent said my parents' house needed a makeover. I was going to paint and de-clutter it. Keep it simple. But I might make a lot more money with your insights. You can just add to the fee you were already planning on charging me. And like I said, I'll have my lawyer draw up a contract, so everything is on the up and up."

This guy was unreal. Or desperate.

"How bad off is the house?" she asked.

He scrunched up his face. "Uh, yeah… I was kind of hoping you'd say yes before I showed it to you."

She chuckled. "That bad?"

"It's clean… It's… Maybe I should show you. And again, it's okay if you say no. But every agent who came through kind of… Never mind, come with me."

He closed the French doors to the pool house.

They went around the enormous pool to a set of sliding glass doors. When he opened the doors, which led into the kitchen, she stopped abruptly. It was very brown. Everything was very brown. The cabinets, the tiles, even the appliances. It was top of the line a few decades ago, but the agents had been right about the room needing an update. Oh, the checkered brown and white wallpaper with a fruit border had to go.

It was hard to meld the idea that the same woman who had the office in the pool house lived in this space.

"So, I can guess what you're thinking. Since she had such good taste with the furnishings and the pool house, why was she living in the past?"

"We have a winner." She gave him a big smile.

"There are some rooms she finished, like the guest rooms upstairs. But she worked all the time. Dad didn't like change or mess, so it took her a while to convince him to let her redo the house. It was the only time I ever saw them argue. I mean, I wasn't home much the last ten years, but every time I came back, she'd done a guest bedroom or bath. There are six of them. But any room Dad lived in, which was most of the downstairs, she was waiting until... And then..."

They'd died. So sad. It made her want to help him even more.

He showed her the rest of the house. The furnishings were lovely, but as they went from room to room, she knew of ways to freshen them up. Most of it wouldn't cost too much.

"Are there wood floors under the carpet?" There was a lot of carpet. Most of it the short, taupe, shag type.

"I think so. The house has been here for over a hundred years." Indeed, and those floors had been protected for a long time. She had a feeling they'd be in great shape.

"So, Matt. I can help you, but since we're being honest, I should tell you that I'm not accredited. I went to college for design. But I dropped out my last year." Much to the chagrin of her parents. She couldn't blame them for being upset. They believed she had a hard time finishing things, and they weren't always wrong.

Then there was her brother—nope. She wouldn't think about that now. She needed to focus. Worrying about the past and what might have been was something she didn't do anymore.

"Are you saying this might be too much?" He looked as if maybe he was going to take back his offer. She couldn't blame him, either. They were standing at the breakfast bar.

"No. I'm saying that I don't want to pretend to be something I'm not. I can do this job, all of it. Your river house, this place and what's in it as well as what's in storage. But I want you to understand what you're getting. I mean, for all you know, I'm some chick who worked at a diner until yesterday and then decided she could decorate."

He crossed his arms and then cocked his head as if he was thinking hard about what she'd said. "Nah. I trust you. Besides, you knew all those details about the furniture and you still handed over all that cash."

She chuckled and folded her arms across her chest. "You really are desperate."

"You have no idea." As if he'd only then understood what he'd just said, he held up his hands in surrender. "I mean, with the houses. I'm…good…with the other stuff."

"Listen, I've just drowned my phone, which had a lot of my portfolio on it, but if you have a laptop, I can show you some pictures of rooms I did before I got to Nashville. I worked at a couple of design firms in Italy and Paris. That's why I left school—to travel the world for inspiration."

"I believe you," he said. "You don't have to prove anything to me."

Right then, a burden lifted off her shoulders. For years, she'd been trying to do just that, whether it was to herself or her parents or her bosses. But Matt had already accepted her for who she was.

"Thanks. It's been a long time since someone has been so kind, or even believed in me. So thanks. Just... thanks."

Why wouldn't her mouth remain closed? So embarrassing.

What is wrong with me? With Matt she was either tongue-tied or couldn't quit jabbering.

I'm tired. And he's hot. Anyone would be confused around all of that sexy man energy. Besides, when was the last time she'd met a guy who was that caring?

Pretty much never. Guys she met always seemed to want something from her.

And while Matt needed help, she knew he was one of the good ones.

"So, you'll stay in the pool house and advise me with this monstrosity of a house? You can add it to your portfolio. Come on, if you can make this a showplace, that ought to get you jobs anywhere."

"The bones are here, and your mom did make a good start upstairs." A wall of tired hit her and she yawned. "And yes, I'll take you up on the pool house, at least for tonight."

The grin on his face made her heart skip a beat.

"Great. We should change the sheets on the bed. I

cleaned all the linens—they're in the closet upstairs. I'll get sheets and towels for you."

"Matt…" She put a hand on his arm. "I slept at a truck stop last night, and I haven't had a proper shower in two days. Old sheets aren't a problem. I'll be fine."

"I'll get the sheets, anyway. And then I'll carry your stuff in from the truck."

She smiled as he took off. He was a good guy. A really good one.

Now, if only she could keep her hands off him.

He's a client. Yes, albeit a fit, good-looking one. But she wouldn't screw this up. Too much depended on it.

5

COFFEE. MATT NEEDED loads of it. Maybe a dump truck full. Most of the night he'd spent thinking about Chelly. About how easy it had been to invite her into his life. How much he wanted her near him. Wrong. That was the last thing she needed—him being possessive.

Having her around would be challenging enough.

Did he need some wandering woman who looked like an angel making his life more complicated? She would, of that he had no doubt, but he hadn't been able to stop himself.

Part of her appeal was her strength. She didn't want handouts, and it was tough for her to accept his kindness. If she'd been greedy or asked for a favor, he might not have been as accepting. But she hadn't asked for anything.

She was a complication. After his last tour, and with everything that had happened with his parents, he should want space. Time alone to get himself together. For his life to make sense again.

He brushed a hand over his face. "What was I think-ing?" he said to his reflection in the mirror.

That you wanted her to be safe. Not only was she a knockout, she was also smart and funny. Last night she'd shown him her portfolio. He didn't know anything about design, but the rooms she'd done were great. Some were busy, lots of patterns and furniture, but most of them were casual spaces where it felt like you could put your feet up. They were neat and very organized. In some ways he'd expected everything to have her kind of free-spirited style, but what she did and how she looked were totally different.

He chuckled.

When he'd used the word *nice*, her eyebrow went up. That was probably a bad thing to say about what she'd done. Maybe he should research design lingo on the internet so he didn't offend her before they got started.

Something told him the peace he craved was going to be disturbed while Chelly was around. Maybe he was more like his dad than he thought. He'd never under-stood his father's reluctance to let his mom fix things up, apart from his dad hating change.

Just like you do.

He tried not to think of that.

Normally, he had Sundays off, but his team was doing test runs on the Apaches, so he had to go into the office to check on their training for a bit. And he needed to check with the lead mechanics about their most recent orders. Most of what he did these days was administrative; he missed getting his hands on his favorite machines. He still had a chance to fly them, but didn't get to work on the birds as often as he liked.

After making coffee, he wrote Chelly a note that he planned on sticking to the door of the pool house. But when he got there, he noticed the curtains were up and she wasn't around.

For a minute, he wondered if she'd left. Maybe the job had been too much. Or maybe she hadn't been comfortable here.

But her truck was in the garage. That was when he heard something upstairs in the apartment.

"Chelly?"

"Yeah," she replied. He followed her voice and found her in the apartment above the garage. There was even more furniture than the last time he'd been up here.

"Matt! I'm so excited for you. This is like hidden treasure. You aren't going to have to buy a thing for your new place," she said. She sat on a chair in the middle of the room. Her hair was piled on top of her head, and she had a notebook and pen in her hands.

"What?"

"Furniture." She gestured around her. "I bet your mom bought all of this to go into the house. She was probably waiting to sort through it first. There's a new dining suite, couches and chairs. I keep saying this, but she had amazing taste.

"Also, I found these in the desk drawer in her office. I hope you don't mind that I snooped. But I had a feeling...well, here, I'll show you." She waved him over.

He was hesitant at first, not sure how he felt about

her going through his mother's things. It seemed wrong. Maybe not wrong, but a violation of his mom's privacy.

She glanced up at him and cocked her head. "Shoot. I did it again. I promise you, it was out of excitement. I lay there all night wondering what her vision might have been. And then at about three this morning it dawned on me that she probably had lists or drawings. In the center drawer I found this."

Curiosity took over, and he moved toward her. It was dumb for him to be mad about his mom's stuff. It wasn't like she would care at this point. "It's okay."

"No. It isn't. But you'll forgive me when you see this." She opened the notebook and showed him. It was the kitchen, their kitchen, only totally different.

"Wow."

"I know. The only thing I might do differently is the blue on the cabinets. I'd either go with white or a lighter wood—maybe maple. Or then make sure the walls are also light so it's not so dark in there. If you were keeping the house, it'd be different. But you want a neutral palette so buyers can imagine themselves in there."

"That makes sense."

"I'd also move the sink so that you can see out the window while doing dishes. I mean, there's a dishwasher, but it's nice when you're cleaning up to have a view. And the plumbing is already over there on that side of the room, so it's a matter of shifting things around— nothing too major. I can get an estimate on the cost for you. But if you have to do dishes, staring out into that beautiful backyard of yours isn't such a bad thing."

"Okay."

She bit her lip again. That was another one of her signs she was nervous. "If you don't like something, I need you to be honest with me. I tend to get very…uh, involved. Or if you don't want to spend that kind of money, I get it. Really, I do. We can stick to basic updates with paint and maybe uncovering those wood floors. I want you to get top dollar, and kitchens and bathrooms are your big sellers. People love family spaces, so if we knock down the wall between the kitchen and den in the back you've got one big area."

His mind couldn't quite comprehend it all. He understood what she was saying, but he was a visual person. It was easier if he could see drawings.

"You hate it. That's fine. We don't have to knock down any walls," she said. Then she took the pencil from her hair and started chewing on the end. Never in his life was he as jealous of anything, let alone a pencil, but he was now. How would those lips feel…?

Get your brain out of the gutter.

"No. No. It's good. But maybe you could come up with a plan," he said and then cleared his throat. "Show me everything that needs to be done, and I can make a budget that will work. I need to see things first." Not that he was averse to spending money, but he was careful. He didn't want to put too much into this place that he wouldn't recoup, because his eye was on the river house.

"That's what I'm working on. By the end of today, I'll have diagrams for all the changes. But with the budget, that might take me a couple of days. I need to research local tradesmen. Who's the best and cheapest tile layer, so we get the most value for your money."

It was all a bit overwhelming and fast. But then that was why she was here. Still, the idea of handing all of this off to a stranger was tough. Made him nervous and a little tense.

"Lists work great for me. As well, I'd like to look over everything before you hire anyone. That sort of thing."

"Okay. I'll get everything together for you."

"Sounds good. I need to get to the base, but I appreciate everything you're doing."

"Oh, of course. Sorry. And I'm jabbering on." She stood then, her shorts riding high on her legs.

He tried hard not to notice, but those legs were killer. So tan and long, even though she wasn't that tall. Maybe five-five. But those legs were more than half of her and ran straight into her very nice—

"No, it's fine. Just wanted to let you know that there's coffee in the kitchen. And I made you some eggs and bacon. The plate is in the fridge. I bought a new microwave, the one on the counter. The built-in one—if you value your life—don't try it. Feel free to use the computer in Mom's office. I left you the password and the internet code. Oh, and there's a landline. Next to it there's a pad of paper with my cell number and other info just in case you need anything—"

She laughed, and then she put her hand on his arm and heat seared straight to his cock.

He had to go.

"Matt, I'll be fine. I promise. But thank you. I'm very

excited about the coffee and breakfast." She followed him down the stairs.

"Okay. I'll be back around dinnertime." He opened the garage door and then rolled his bike out. He waved.

That was awkward. Mainly because he'd had this urge to kiss her. She'd pursed her lips again while he'd been rambling and all he could think about was what she'd taste like. Strawberries. He was betting she tasted like strawberries.

"Are you okay?" Her voice penetrated his thick skull. He was standing in the middle of the driveway holding the handlebars of the bike, staring off into space.

"Yep. See you later." Then he climbed on the bike and took off.

Chelly was a force. He understood that now. A chaotic wind had just blown in, and he wasn't at all sure he'd survive.

AWKWARD.

And this is why you don't spend the night at a client's house. At least she hadn't slept with him. Not that she hadn't thought about it. More than once. Okay, at least a hundred times. She'd never admit it to him, but that was the main reason she couldn't sleep. Never in her life had she met a man like Matt. Compassionate, funny, bright.

He was the step-up-to-the-plate, do-whatever-it-takes-to-get-the-job-done kind of awesome. Then there was the beautiful packaging. The way his abs moved toward those cut-in hips.

She hit herself in the head with the notebook. "No.

No. No. No. He's a client. Off-limits. Keep it professional."

Besides, he couldn't be that perfect. No one was.

After closing the garage door, she went in search of the coffee. If she kept her mind on work, and goodness there was a lot of it to do, maybe she could quit thinking about the hot Marine.

As if.

She poured a cup of coffee and then opened the fridge to find her eggs.

The man made her breakfast.

She'd fallen hard for guys who had done less. But that was the old Chelly. The new one was careful with her heart. Protective of herself. There would be no men until she had her business up and running.

Once she had her breakfast, she powered up his mom's computer and was delighted to find it had one of her favorite design programs on it. She wasn't much into social media, except for Pinterest. She was trying to remember where she'd seen some sea-green-and-gray throw pillows. In a few seconds she found the store and wrote down the cost. There wouldn't be much she'd need in terms of accessories. His mother had bought most of those, as well.

Working on his mom's house was an honor, and one Chelly didn't take lightly. It was an opportunity to really make his mother's dream come true—even if it was a bit late.

"I'll do you proud," she whispered after she shut down the computer. She wanted to start cataloging everything in the main house. And then she'd hit the garage.

SHE WAS IN the garage when the door started to open. She jumped. The thrum of the engine from Matt's bike quelled her nerves. She hadn't realized how much time had passed, and boy, did she have some good news for him.

"Hey," he said after shutting off the engine. "How's it going?"

"Good. I've made a lot of progress."

He nodded. "I brought home some steaks and potatoes." He pulled the grocery bags from the storage compartments on his bike. "And some stuff for salad. I thought I'd grill, if that's okay?"

Her stomach chose that moment to grumble. They laughed. "I'm not going to argue about food. I'm kind of dusty and dirty. Why don't I get cleaned up and I'll help with the salad. I tend to blow up baked potatoes, but I'm a great chopper."

An hour and a half later they were sitting by the pool. Her belly so full, her eyes were droopy. "That was good, Matt. If you ever want to give up on the helicopter thing, you could make it as a chef."

"It's not exactly an art form to cook a steak on a grill."

She waved away the comment. "I've had a lot of not-so-great steaks. That was definitely art. Oh, that reminds me. I devised a timetable for you." She slid out a spreadsheet toward him. "I'm not so great with these, but I had a feeling you might be a fan."

When he didn't say anything, she glanced up to find him smiling at her. One of those pantie-falling-off smiles that stole her breath away.

He's a client.

Right. Right. "I'm still investigating costs. But this is a rough idea of the timetable and prices. But I'll have something more solid for you in a few days."

He nodded and took the printout from her. "I don't know if it helps but that friend I mentioned earlier, the one who is engaged to the designer, he said she'd be willing to talk things over with you. Mari's nice. I can't remember the name of the company, but I wrote down her number."

She sat back. Hiding her disappointment, she gave him a tight smile. "Oh, would you rather have her design everything? That's understandable. Now that you've had time to think about it, I'm not surprised."

His hand covered hers, and her fingers tingled. "No, that's not at all what I meant. I trust you. I just meant, she would likely know the best people to work with on this sort of project. She was key when I was trying to talk to the architect about the river house. He and I did not speak the same language. I was getting pretty frustrated.

"And I thought it could save you time if you asked her for those contacts you were talking about."

Oh. *Oh. Why do I always go straight to he probably doesn't want me?*

"Thanks," she said hesitantly. "I appreciate you reaching out. I'll give her a call tomorrow."

His eyebrows furrowed. "You don't have to. I wasn't trying to tell you what to do. Although, you should probably be ready for that sort of thing. I pretty much always think my way is better. But with this, I thought, since you haven't been in town very long—"

"That's sweet. I appreciate it." His hand was warm on hers and strong. She turned her hand up and squeezed his.

She had a feeling he really was just trying to be nice about it all. "I'm not used to people wanting to help."

"I think maybe you haven't been hanging out with the right people."

She laughed. "That is so true." Pulling her hand from his, she stood. "I'm going to do the dishes."

He started to argue, but she held up a hand. "No arguments. Go do whatever it is you do this time of night. I'm doing the dishes. Then I'm crashing big-time. It's been a long day."

He picked up his plate and followed her into the kitchen. "I rented a trailer for this weekend. Since the garage is full, I thought I'd get rid of or store whatever needs to be out of here for the project to begin. If you can make a list, then I'll know what needs to be done. Uh...I'm kind of a big fan of lists and order. I mentioned that, right?"

"Right. So we'll keep the clutter to a minimum, but there are going to be some days when you come home and the place is a wreck. That's part of rebuilding." She snapped her fingers. "I could fix up the apartment above the garage for you. Use some of the pieces that are there and maybe store the rest until the place is finished."

"You don't think I'll be able to live in the main house while people are working? I don't understand."

He leaned on the breakfast bar.

"You might. But it's going to be a lot of dust and dirt. Um. Oh, and I was going to ask if I can hang in the pool house a couple more days. It would make it easier to get all the furniture and antiques cataloged. And my friend should be back from her impromptu honeymoon. Though I haven't exactly figured out how I'm going to get in touch with her. Her email bounced. I'm about to give up on her."

He frowned again. "I'd prefer it if you were around to oversee things. And before you suggest it, I don't want any rent, so put that money toward your business. You'd be doing me a favor by being here on the work site."

Was she dreaming? "Are you sure? I mean, I'll do my best to stay out of your hair and keep the work from bugging you too much."

"Sure. My moving into the space over the garage is a good idea. Though it seems like a lot to get that place into something livable."

"Not really. Once we get the unnecessary furniture out, it's a matter of tidying and cleaning. I can have it ready by the end of the week."

"Or you could move in there, and I can take the pool house," he said.

She grinned. "I don't see you living with all that white and ruffles. And you on that daybed? Uh. No. I promise I can get the apartment fixed up. That'll give you some idea of what I can do for the house."

He gazed at her skeptically. "Okay. Well, I'm going to run upstairs and shower. Thanks for doing the dishes."

After putting his plate on the counter, he left.

She absentmindedly washed the few things they'd messed up, and dried and put them away.

Was she taking on too much? Probably. But she wanted

him to be comfortable during the construction and design phases, and she had a feeling this was the best way.

She checked the time and then pulled the number from her pocket. If she was going to do this, she would need to know the best people for the job, and that meant taking the first step.

Picking up the landline, she dialed the number he'd given her.

HE FELT LIKE a heel leaving her down there with the dishes, but he needed time away from her. Time to breathe. When she was around sometimes he got confused. The shower was on warm, but he needed it cold. The way she'd smiled at him, it was so simple and sweet and made his cock rock hard.

That was the last thing he needed. The last thing she needed.

His cock was in his hand before he could think about it. Wrong, so wrong to do this with her downstairs. She might hear him, but he couldn't stop. When she'd bent over to put that plate in the dishwasher... He was strangely obsessed with her ass. Usually, he was more of a boob man, which she also had in spades.

He needed to get laid. But not by her. No. They were working together and she was a bona fide mess. He didn't do messes.

He wanted a solid woman with a good head on her shoulders. Not that she didn't have a good head on her shoulders for the design stuff she did. But he was worried about her managing a project this big. He'd let her believe she was in charge, but he'd keep an eye on things.

I barely know her and she's overseeing one of the biggest projects in my life.

What had he been thinking? He should have told her that they were going too fast and that he needed time. But he didn't really have time. If he wanted the money to finish the river house, he had to get his parents' home sold. That wasn't going to happen without updates and improvements.

And she'd shown him everything she wanted to accomplish. It was good. Everything would be fine.

He pumped his cock harder. He just had to keep things professional between them. This was business.

As he came for a second time, he turned the water to cold.

Yes. Just business.

6

CHELLY CHECKED HER new phone one more time. The designer had texted her the address to the coffee shop, which was in a charming little neighborhood in downtown Corpus. Her hand shook a little.

Why am I so nervous? The designer, Mari, had been kind, especially when she'd mentioned she was a friend of Matt's and was helping him with his house.

Two women entered the coffee shop; one was dressed in black jeans and a simple black cotton T-shirt, and had about six earrings in her right ear and dark purple streaks running through her brunette hair. The other woman was dressed in a more sophisticated yet fun dress with matching shoes and accessories. Her curly hair had been tamed with a cute headband.

The one in the dress cocked her head and pointed at her. "Are you Chelly?"

Dressed in worn jeans and an eighties rock band T-shirt, Chelly almost said no. But since when did she care what people thought of how she dressed. She nodded.

"Oh, see," said the other woman. "I told you she'd be cool if she was from Nashville."

Chelly stood and held out her hand. "Hi, it's great to meet you both."

Dress Lady took her hand and shook it. "I'm Mari, and this is my former assistant turned partner just last week, and more important, best friend, Abbott. We run the design company together."

"Can I get you guys some coffee?" Chelly asked. She didn't have much cash, but they were doing her a big favor.

"It's already on the way," Abbott said. "This is our place. Our order starts as soon as we walk in the door. And we designed the place, so free coffee for life."

"Wow. Well, it's very quaint and homey." Chelly laughed and held up her cup. "I may become a regular, as well. This is good stuff."

"I know, right?" Mari said. "We can't exist without it. They have the strongest coffee in town, and they use fresh cream. So good. And good to know you're one of us. Some folks can't handle it."

"Oh, I'm of the stronger the better persuasion when it comes to coffee."

"You said it, sister." Abbott grinned. "So how did you end up here?"

Chelly bit her lip. "That's kind of a long story. None of it shows me in a great light. Wrong man, dead-end job and I needed a fresh start. Got here and my friend I was supposed to stay with ran off and got married. I ended up meeting Matt and, well, his house is a gold mine. I'm in the process of starting a repurposing and design business—and wow, I'm blabbering."

"Brody's my fiancé and he says Matt can't stop talking about you. How good your ideas are." Mari smiled.

Did he? That was sweet.

"Hmm, he's the same guy who thought a Chippendale étagère was a twenty-dollar bookshelf, so you might not want to put too much into that."

They laughed again.

"Men." Abbott shook her head. "Did he really?"

"Yep. I ended up selling it for five hundred, but I could have gotten more for him if we'd gone to an auction."

"Thank goodness you showed up when you did," Mari said. "Brody told me how much money you made him. I'd emailed him a couple of good estate sale companies but he was determined to do it on his own."

"I know. I'm trying to get him top dollar to help with his renovations and with his other house."

Mari nodded. "So tell us what you need."

"Being new to town, like really new, I don't know anyone when it comes to tradespeople. I don't expect you to share yours. Designers can be proprietary about that sort of thing. But I made up a list, and I was hoping maybe you guys could go over it with me?"

"Oh, hon. We're happy to share all of our secrets with any friend of Matt's," Abbott said. She waggled her eyebrows. "That Marine is jaw-dropping. He's got the best bod ever."

Chelly smiled, but there was a slight stab of jealousy. How dumb was that? Matt was single and free—and a client. She had to stop thinking about him that way.

She agreed. "I can't argue with any of that."

Mari was eyeing her in that *so is it more than business* look.

Chelly held up her hands. "I'm so not in the market for a new man. This is a job, a welcome one. I'm not going to complicate it with that sort of thing. I can appreciate a hot guy without touching. It's my new superpower."

It had taken all of her strength to keep her hands off his abs.

"I look at Matt as kind of a little brother, even though we're almost the same age. He's been really great about helping with Brody's classes while he's going back and forth for his dad's cancer treatments in Houston."

"Oh. How's his dad doing?"

"So far, so good," Mari said. "But Matt's been terrific filling in. And he comes over to the house a lot for dinner when Brody's in town. So we've gotten to know him pretty well. Why don't you show us what you've done up till now?"

A while went by and eventually Mari stood. Abbott did the same. "Chelly, I've got to head out for a final run-through with some clients," Mari told her. "But you should be all set, and if you have any questions let me know. Tell Matt to bring you to the mixer at the CO's on Saturday. You need to meet people, and that whole crew is really nice."

"I'll be too busy with the job, but thanks." She shouldn't spend more time with Matt, especially if it wasn't job related. The attraction was already too strong.

Mari laughed. "We'll see. No matter what, you've

got my cell number and Abbott's. If you need us, call, okay? And when you talk to Rafe about the tile, tell him you want the Mari McGuire special. Don't be shy. You can pass the savings on to Matt. I always look out for my friends."

"Done," Chelly said as she waved goodbye to the women. Her head was whirling with possibilities. She had several more calls to make, but she wanted to grab some groceries for dinner. While she wasn't the best cook, she could make a mean shrimp scampi.

And she wanted a swim. She thought about heading to the beach, but maybe she could work by the pool at Matt's and kill two birds with one stone.

It wasn't long before she had the tradesmen set for the project. Work would begin a week from Tuesday. Well, once Matt approved everything. It was time consuming making up his lists, but she did it. And she drew out all the plans. And the project date would give them time to clear out some of the space, and she would have time to repurpose some of the furniture and figure out the storage situation.

She turned on the radio and pushed the button for the music to play out at the pool. Then she changed into her red and white polka dot bikini. It was superrevealing, but she'd always loved the suit. And Matt wouldn't be home for a few hours.

After swimming several laps, she dropped down onto one of the lounge chairs with her notebook and started writing her thoughts regarding the kitchen, dining area, family room and formal living area. She drew the entry three different ways and then wondered if she could convince Matt to open up the wall off the stairs. It would make the entry a lot more inviting.

While she'd been nervous before, she was now getting excited. This was coming together. And she could do it for a lot less than she'd thought in the beginning.

Though she'd worked at many design firms, she'd done all of this as an assistant. Until today, she'd never had the chance to manage a large project on her own.

Stay focused. Take one step at a time.

For the first time in months, Chelly's confidence was back. It didn't hurt that Mari and Abbott had thought her design plan was solid and even innovative. "It's so fresh, exactly what that old house needs." Mari had used those exact words.

She could do this. And start her business, as well. She had a habit of taking on too much at once, but it would be different because this time she loved what she was doing.

This time things will be different.

FOCUS WASN'T SOMETHING that was ever a problem for Matt. When it was time to get the task done, he was the man. He was a Marine. But even the toughest Marine would be distracted by the sight before him.

Chelly in a red-and-white bikini, her ass firm enough to entice him to want to touch. It was fine. And just like that he was hard again.

He'd been so determined to keep this friendly between them. Would it be the first mission he'd fail?

It should help that she wasn't his type at all. Well, she was every man's type. She was gorgeous, had a great sense of humor, was creative, had a good heart...but he was ready to settle down and have a family. To train helicopter navigators and mechanics and lead a quiet life.

She was all about chasing rainbows and getting her business going. Not that he didn't want a wife who had her own interests, her own mind, her own likes and desires.

He did. He appreciated strong women; he was attracted to strong women just like Chelly.

But ones who were ready for the kind of life he wanted.

She was a free spirit. He respected her independence and would keep his distance. They had a work relationship only.

But damn, the woman was fine.

His phone started ringing and he almost dropped the thing in the pool. "Hello?"

Chelly's head whipped around and she waved at him.

She'd caught him looking, but she smiled so maybe she wasn't too mad.

"Hey buddy, it's Mari."

"What's up? You ready to give up on the old man and see what it's like on the dark side?"

Chelly frowned. Had she heard him, and why would she care?

Mari laughed.

"You know I just can't quit him. But if ever I do, you're the first one I'll call. Right after that hot CO of you-alls."

"Hey, enough of that," he heard Brody say in the background.

"Anyhoo, that's why I'm calling. You should bring Chelly to the swim party on Saturday."

He'd forgotten about that. They had team-building events at least once a month hosted by the CO. This one was just for officers and their significant others.

"Uh. That's not really—I mean, we're not dating. So that's not appropriate." He headed through the sliding glass doors into the kitchen and set his sunglasses on the bar. "She's working for me, or with me. I'm not really sure what you say. That would be wrong, misleading. Besides, we're going to be busy that day."

"Yeah, yeah. But she can come as your friend. Since she's new to town, I thought it would give her a chance to meet people. You're a Marine, you know how it is every time you get sent somewhere new. You're a tough guy. But she's trying to start a business and she needs to network. It will be good for her. From what I could gather, it sounds like she had a tough time in Nashville. It would be good for her to meet some nice people. Nothing wrong with that, right?"

Mari had a way about her, and Brody was right, it was really hard to say no to the woman. He realized he had that same problem with Chelly.

"I already told her about it, so she's expecting you to ask. And I got the CO's approval. We finished the remodel on his house and he wants to show it off. I'm also hiring the caterers and decorating since you know who is out of town."

You know who was the CO's niece. A professional troublemaker. Word was she was chasing poor Ben, another instructor on the base and one of his friends.

"Okay. I'll ask her, but she's pretty hands-on with everything here at the house. And they're supposed to be laying the foundation for the river house this weekend."

"Oh, I didn't realize that was happening so soon."

"I've changed a few things around, instead of trying to connect everything. Anyway, I'm still not sure. I've made it to the last two of the CO's events, so I was kind of thinking it would be okay if I skipped this one."

She sighed. "It's up to you. But I feel sorry for Chelly not knowing anyone. You really should introduce her around. That's what a friend would do."

Matt rubbed his temple. That was the problem. While he didn't want to admit it, he had a feeling Chelly would be really popular among his friends, none of whom were good enough for her. "I guess we can come by for a little bit."

"Great." Mari's voice brightened. "We'll see you Saturday."

He pushed the off button and sat his phone next to his sunglasses.

"Hey," Chelly said, "you're home early. I can get dinner started. I was going to make you some shrimp scampi."

"Uh, that sounds nice. That," he said and pointed to the phone, "was Mari. She thinks you should come to the swim party on Saturday at my CO's house."

She bit her lip. "Oh."

"You're probably busy with the house. I told her that, but she doesn't take no for an answer. I can go by myself and explain you couldn't make it."

"Whatever you think's best," she said, but she was frowning.

He'd bungled it. Probably made her feel bad.

"Unless you want to go? She said it might be good for you to let folks know about your new business. I just don't want you to feel like you have to go because I asked."

"She mentioned that earlier, but it's your work thing. I'd understand if you didn't want me to go."

She was making this easy for him. Was she embarrassed to go with him for some reason? He was more worried about offending her, but maybe she didn't want to hang out with him outside of working on the house?

"It's okay with me if you'd like to come," he said. "We're friends, at least that is how I think of us. So it's fine with me."

"Then, yes. I didn't want to impose or anything. I mean, we are going to have lots to do that day, but it would be fun to meet other people."

They were dancing around one another, trying to protect each other's feelings.

"Look, I want you to feel comfortable. And you should meet the people I work with." He'd just decided that. "And Mari and Brody will be there, so you'll know at least two other people. It's a swim party."

Her eyes widened. "I'll probably need to go buy a suit."

Matt swallowed hard. "What's wrong with the one you're wearing?"

"This thing? I've had it since I was a freshman in college. It's not fit to wear in public. I'm a little embarrassed you saw me in it. But we're friends so no big deal, right?"

Yes. Friends. Though a friend probably wouldn't want to take her on that lounger...

Dude, she's looking at you.

"Absolutely. So Saturday at four p.m. I guess is when it starts."

"Cool. I'm going to go make some calls. I'll get dinner started in about a half hour."

"Great. That's great," he said as she turned and went back through the sliding glass doors.

He watched as she left.

Shower. Yep. He needed another cold one.

7

ON THURSDAY NIGHT Matt met some of the guys at the pub close to his house to watch the Rangers baseball game. They tried to get together a couple times a month. The psychiatrist who'd treated Brody for PTSD had said it was good for him to spend time with like minds. Matt had to agree. They'd all been through hell in their own way.

He sat at the bar with his untouched beer. He wasn't sure he could handle another night alone with Chelly. The last few days had been torture. He'd taken more cold showers in one week than any man should in a life-time. She was so beautiful, but it was more than that.

There was a sweetness about her, yet she was tough. And he wasn't sure he'd ever met a more laid-back, open-minded person. He'd spent so many years in the military that he was used to being around various kinds of people. Marines worked hard, put everything on the line, but they also played hard. One thing he and Chelly did have in common was traveling. She'd been all over the world. So had he.

But she would go places with only a backpack and a few dollars. She'd find work and study the culture of wherever she was, until she was ready to move on. It took a lot of guts for someone to travel like that, never knowing where their next dollar or meal was coming from—or where they'd be living.

Cheers went up around him and he focused again on the game. "Can't believe he hit another homerun," Brody said beside him.

"That's three this game," Ben said from the other side of the table. "Dude is on fire."

"Yep," Matt added so they wouldn't know he'd spent the last twenty minutes thinking about Chelly. He did that a lot lately. If she was the kind of woman who would settle down, he'd try to—what? Woo her? He'd known her barely a week.

Even if he wanted to make a move, she wasn't ready. He'd garnered a lot of information about her ex, who sounded like a possessive jerk.

Though he kind of understood why the jerk would want to hang on to Chelly. She was the stuff a man's dreams were made of.

Game. Focus on the game. You came here to get away from thinking about her.

"Mari says that designer you hired is your new girl-friend," Brody stated.

Matt nearly knocked over his beer, only his quick reflexes kept it from pouring all over the dark wood. "What?"

"You're dating, and these are her words, 'a super designer with a supermodel body.' So who is she?"

Supermodel? She was attractive, but Matt was into the whole package. She was as good-hearted as she was beautiful. And, yes, he was definitely into her.

"Not a girlfriend," he said. "She's just helping me with my parents' house, and maybe a little with the river house."

"Right. That's why you've been staring at your beer all night instead of watching the game, because you're not dating." He made air quotes on the last three words.

"Marines don't do air quotes. And, yes, she's gorgeous. Probably one of the nicest people I've ever met, but it's strictly business between us."

He had to keep reminding himself of that.

"Uh-huh. Business."

"Monkey business," Ben added. "Are you bringing her to the swim party? If she's not into you, maybe she'll be into a good-looking Marine. Women love me."

"Yeah, just ask the CO's niece, Carissa," Matt threw out. That woman had gone after just about every guy on the base; he figured it was mostly to keep the CO on his toes.

Ben shook his head. "I took her to that party at Brody's because the CO asked me to. He wanted me to keep an eye on her. I told you, we're just friends. She scares me a little, that one. I like to think I could handle any woman, but that one—she's stunning, but scary. Way too much woman for me."

"Chelly and I are just friends, too."

"Right. You keep telling yourself that, brother,"

Brody said. "That's how Mari and I started out, and you see where that ended up."

His friend was engaged, and it had happened really fast.

"You having second thoughts?" Matt asked.

"No. Not at all," Brody said quickly. "If I had my way, we'd have been married months ago."

"So how many times a day do you think about her?" Ben asked.

"About Chelly? Or Mari?" Matt joked, trying to get them off the Chelly track.

"Hey, if you want to die, say that again," Brody said, but he wasn't serious. Instead, he grinned.

He was happy for his friend. Someday, Matt wanted to find the right girl and settle down, and he could only hope to be as happy as Mari and Brody.

"Well, just know, if you don't treat Mari right, I'm next in line. She told me on the phone the other day."

"If you weren't trying to deflect away from Chelly so hard, I might have had to punch your face," Brody said.

"For the last time, she's a—"

"Friend," Ben and Brody said at the same time. Then they fist bumped across Matt.

"You guys suck."

"So she's just not into you?" Brody asked.

"What?" Matt growled. "Do we have to talk about this now?" This was not getting his mind off the Chelly problem.

"Okay, you do have it bad." Ben chugged his beer and then signaled the bartender for another one.

"Does she know you're interested?" Brody asked.

How could she not? She caught him looking at her so many times it was embarrassing. "Doesn't matter," he said. "I thought we were here to watch the game."

"All right, brother. All right." Brody patted him on the back. "Marines are stubborn."

"True that," Ben said and they clinked bottles.

Chelly had made it clear that she'd just gotten out of a bad relationship and she wasn't looking for anything new. But what would happen if Matt let her know that he was interested?

And then what? Hot sex. He'd make those fantasies he'd had in the shower come to life.

No. No. Business. That was what this was.

He chugged his beer.

Right. Business.

THE GARAGE DOOR opening pulled Chelly away from her notebook where she'd been sketching ideas for Matt's river house. He'd shown her the finalized plans the night before, and the ideas had been flowing like crazy. This was what her brain did when she was in creative mode—went a million miles a minute. And she was definitely in creative mode.

Earlier she'd tried to work on her website but she'd reached a point where she needed someone who wrote code.

And then there was the whole security aspect of a shopping website that she hadn't counted on. It wasn't just a matter of taking photos and posting them. She needed a way for people to check out securely, and a way to protect that info. Every day there was news about how hackers stole people's personal information, and companies that were being sued for it.

That kind of buyer protection was beyond her capabilities, and put a damper on her plan to make some quick cash by putting Matt's mom's stuff up for sale. He'd given her carte blanche to sell the extra things in storage any way she saw fit.

And she'd planned on repurposing some of the junkier pieces she had in her truck to start her site. The rest she was farming out to different auction houses, ones that didn't charge an arm and a leg. She'd also offer a few things on another online retail site just to mix it up.

There was a knock on the open doors of the pool house. She liked that he was unfailingly polite. Even though this was his property, he gave her privacy. And he never overstepped. Oh, and there was the fact that he was always feeding her and looking out for her.

"Come on in," she said.

"Everything okay?" he asked as he stepped through the door. She still couldn't get over how hot Matt was. Tonight he wore jeans and a black T-shirt. His muscled chest pulling the cotton tight, and those narrow hips—she'd been thinking about what it would be like to climb on him and kiss him until she couldn't remember her name.

But she wouldn't.

Sex would complicate things.

"Yep. Did you have fun? Who won?"

"Rangers did. What are you working on?"

She pulled the sketchbook to her chest. "You won't get mad if I show you something, right?"

"I'd never get mad at you," he said. He was so sincere, her heart did a little double thump. The man was dangerous.

She motioned him to come around the desk where she was sitting. He did, and pulled up the ottoman from the chair next to the desk and sat down.

"Okay, so these are just ideas and if you hate them, it's okay."

He frowned. "I thought we'd already decided on everything for the house."

"We have," she said. "But these are your ideas for *your* house."

"The river house?"

She nodded. Then she held out her sketchbook and flipped back a few pages. "There are about six pages of ideas."

He took the sketches from her and thumbed through the pages slowly. The man had to be a great poker player, because she could not read his face. He made it to the last page, and then he turned back to the beginning and started again.

She realized she'd been holding her breath and let it out. Did he hate them?

"I like the color scheme with the browns and the blues on the second one in the family room," he said. "I wanted the focus to be on the view, and you did that. It sort of blends everything. It's comfortable."

"That's good, right? Comfortable."

"Yeah," he said. "Is this some of the stuff from my mom's storage?"

"Yes. I know you're spending more on this house

than you'd planned. I wasn't sure how much you'd planned on spending for the river house. You said you wanted to keep things simple, more minimal. So I went with that."

He smiled. "It's like you were in my brain. You got this from just the little bit we talked about last night? I mean, this is unreal. The only thing I'd change is the couches. I know it sounds like a guy thing, but I really wanted leather. Not that supershiny stuff. But like a light tan, supersoft like an old pair of shoes or a saddle. More because I'll be working outside a lot and fishing. I don't want to have to worry about the furniture when I come in. And I'm planning on getting a dog so I want something easy to clean."

"You're going to get a dog?"

"I've always wanted one. We had a Great Dane when I was a kid. Hank. I loved that dog. I decided when I had enough land for one to run around, I wanted to get another Dane."

"Those dogs are huge."

"Hence the need for a lot of space. Hank was older when we got him so he was fine just hanging around the house. Anyway, other than the leather, if you can work that in, this is pretty close to perfect."

"And here I was worried that you'd be mad. That you'd believe I was trying to take over everything."

"I'm not sure why you would think that. I love everything you do. I mean, uh." He handed her the sketchbook back. "There's something—that is… Uh."

She smiled and put her hand on his. He was so warm and strong. "What is it?"

He stared at their hands as if they were on fire and she pulled hers away. "Sorry," she said.

But he caught her hand and held it in his. "I can't get you out of my head," he said.

Her heart did that weird double thump again. That happened a lot when he was around. "What?" Not her brightest moment, but she couldn't form words. He thought about her?

"You've been through so much—and I don't want to add to your troubles. But I'm having a hard time keeping this just business. You're in my head twenty-four-seven. I'm telling you so that you aren't freaked out when I do this."

And then he leaned forward to kiss her, lightly at first. His lips testing hers. Heat seared from her mouth straight to her core. Yes. She'd been wanting this for days. Heck, ever since she'd laid eyes on him.

But it was wrong. Really wrong.

Then his thumb stroked across her jaw so tenderly, she sighed and opened her mouth to his exploration. He tasted of beer and mint, an odd but tasty combination. Never in her life had a kiss done so much to her body. She thrummed from head to toe.

And then she was lost in him.

When they parted they were both breathing hard.

They stared at each other and then he stood, looking as if he might bolt.

"That was—um, good," she said. "Very, very good."

She wasn't going to do this.

Then he pulled her to him.

Yes, yes she was.

All reason flew out the window when he touched her.

His hand went around to her lower back, his other to her neck, angling her head so he could kiss her again.

"This is a really bad idea," she said right before his lips came down on hers.

After another kiss that made her weak in the knees, she worried she wouldn't be able to stand much longer. His mouth moved to her ear. "You're right. This is a terrible idea. You can tell me to stop, but I'm doing this until you tell me you don't want it." Then he nibbled on her ear, and her body filled with heat.

"Can't lie," she moaned as she pressed herself to him and his hardness pressed into her belly. And yes, there was a whole lot of hardness there.

"Matt," she said, her voice so husky and needy.

"Yes," he answered, as he trailed kisses against her throat.

"If we do this, it won't ruin what we have, right? I need you as my friend."

"Friends," he said. "Yes."

She smiled. "I don't think you're listening to me."

"I've heard every word, but you haven't said stop, so I'm still doing this." His hand slipped into the front of her shorts and went straight to her core. His rough fingers working their magic against her hard nub.

Gasping, she held on to his shoulders. When he slid a finger into her, she threw her head back. "Oh." It was the only word that came to her mind. "Ohhh."

He leaned her against the desk, his focus never wavering.

"Matt," she cried out and shuddered. Never in her

life had she come so quickly. This man. He did it to her. Did it for her.

"So beautiful," he said, nuzzling her neck, and then his teeth were at the lobe of her ear again, as his fingers teased her to the brink once more.

"I need you," she said. "Inside me. Please tell me you have a condom."

He paused and she opened her eyes to look at him.

His eyes were hooded and slightly glazed. "Are you sure?" But the hand that had just brought her pleasure was digging into his pockets.

She couldn't keep the slow grin. "No. But I need you. Tell me you need me, Matt."

"So bad, Chelly," he said. "So bad."

"A Marine who follows orders. You really are some-thing."

He held up the package. "You can say no, of course, but I hope you say yes. I've never wanted anyone as much as you."

That may have been the biggest turn-on yet.

She pulled her shorts and thong off, as well as her top.

He took her in, the expression on his face leaving no worry for her about how much he truly desired her.

"*Yes* is the only word I'll be saying tonight," she told him honestly. Bad idea or not, she needed him. "Are you going to just stand there, or are you going to get naked?"

He was out of his jeans and T-shirt in seconds, and then it was her turn to take a look. The man was a solid wall of muscled perfection, and he was at full attention.

Taking the package from his hand, she ripped it open

with her teeth. Then she rolled the condom down his length. "Last chance." He hissed out the words when she stroked his erection, which grew with her touch. She loved having this kind of effect on him.

"I'm only taking this chance because it's you." Then she scooted onto the desk and reached for him. "Come on, Marine. Let's do this."

He groaned. The tip of him touching her. "Wrap your legs around me, babe."

She did what he asked. His lips found hers as he guided himself into her slowly. He filled her so much, she wasn't sure she could take him all. He pulled out and went a little farther the next time.

She hissed in a breath.

"You're so tight," he whispered. "So tight."

He was being careful with her. But she wasn't in the mood for careful. "More, please," she said, bending back onto her elbows, her bare breasts jutting into the air.

He sucked a nipple, and there was a tingling in her core. The man had the best mouth ever. As they found a powerful rhythm, his hand went back to that hard little nub. Soon she was mindlessly writhing underneath him.

"Matt," she begged.

"Yes, Chelly?"

"Sooo. Good. Sooo." And then she came apart, her body quivering, her muscles tightening. For a second she thought she might pass out from the pleasure, but then he was thrusting, full, heavy strokes, and she could feel herself quickening again.

He might kill her with all these orgasms, but what a way to go.

"You're exquisite, Chelly."

It was all she could do not to cry with joy. Never had she felt so cherished or appreciated. And sure it was just sex, but it was with Matt. And the way he looked at her...

It was everything.

"I'm so close again," she said. "Come with me."

He smiled and then thrust faster. Her mind nearly blacking out again.

"Chelly," he said as he came. "Yes."

And then she was over the edge with him.

Tomorrow. She'd think about the consequences of what they'd just done tomorrow.

For now, she was losing herself in her favorite Marine.

8

MATT STARED AT the woman beside him. She was sound asleep, her strawberry-blond hair a riotous mass framing her face on the pillow. He'd never seen a more beautiful woman. They were cramped on the daybed in the pool house, but he hadn't been able to leave. Or sleep. He had to be at work at zero seven hundred hours, which was quickly approaching. But he couldn't drag himself away.

And it scared him.

She wasn't a forever kind of girl. She'd actually told him that. Said she was too much of a free spirit to ever settle down.

They'd only had sex twice. Yet before she'd fallen asleep, she'd whispered that he was the most talented friend with benefits she'd ever had.

It caught him off guard. He wasn't sure if he should be grateful that she'd thought he was the best. But he was more worried about the fact that the moment she'd had him inside her, he'd been hers. As in, he'd begun to wonder what happened next because he wanted more. Not just sex. Not just friends.

But she didn't want more. He was just kidding himself. If he pushed her, she'd probably run. So he had to play it cool.

Cool? He hadn't gone to get ready for work yet and he already felt lonely. He carefully extricated himself so as not to wake her.

He grabbed his stuff but then stopped to write her a note. But what was he supposed to say? Best sex of my life, thanks? No. His hand hit the mouse on the computer and the screen popped to life. She'd been working on her website. He read a few lines and saw where she was trying to write some code. But she had it wrong. Well, it depended on what exactly she needed, but he could help her with that. He'd had to learn to write code as part of his job in the Corps and had finished his business degree while overseas. But he didn't have the time now to fix it.

If he was late, and he never was, the CO would kick his butt. He scribbled a quick note, and then twenty minutes later he was heading into work, having taken the quickest shower ever.

He was a little nervous about leaving Chelly without talking. But they could discuss things later when he got home. Figure out what this was and move on.

Until then, it was finals for the grunts he'd been training. They'd be taking their flight tests next week. And he had to be on his game.

WHEN HE LATER pulled up to the garage with the U-Haul in tow for the extra furniture, the door was already open. Chelly was there, covered in paint, staring at what used to be the old dresser from his room when he was a kid. He hadn't minded it much then. It was a place to hold his clothes, but Chelly had commented that it was the ugliest piece of furniture she'd ever seen, though it had potential.

He didn't see it then, but he'd helped her move the dresser to the garage so she could work on it just the same. But now, heck, it was barely recognizable. It looked like something out of a magazine. Definitely no longer looked like a dresser. She'd cut off the legs so that it sat lower.

"Is it an entertainment center?"

"Ding, ding, ding, the Marine wins another prize," she called out. Then she bent over to put the lid on the paint can, and Matt forgot to breathe.

"Is that from one of your sketches I saw last night?"

"You win again." She stood up and he noticed the paint she had on her forehead and hands and knees. But she wasn't smiling.

"Did you paint it, or did it paint you?" he joked.

She glanced down at herself. "I tend to be a bit messy when I work, but don't worry. I'll clean everything up in here."

Somehow he'd disappointed her. He could tell from her tone. "You're an artist, and maybe part magician," he said. "Really, Chelly, this could be some high-end piece at a furniture store. It'll go perfect in my family room at the river house."

This time she grinned. "I know, right? I went a little lighter with the dry brush colors and gave it more of a natural look, but in a masculine way. Like you can tell it's furniture for a guy's place."

"Exactly. I really like it. It's perfect for my flat screen. What are you doing with the drawers?"

She bent over again and picked up a sack. She had to stop doing that or his heart might stop. "I found these at a restoration place," she said as she opened the sack and pulled out a rustic-looking handle. "They'll complement the drawers. And it will give it that entertainment-cabinet feel. Plus, you'll have storage for your games or DVDs. Seems everyone's stuff is digital these days, but it's still lots of good storage. The bottom drawers are wide and tall enough that you could store blankets or afghans for the winter months. Not that it ever gets that chilly down here."

He had no idea what an afghan was, but she was right about the weather. The average winter temps were usually in the sixties. But he liked the idea of snuggling on the couch with her. Stop. He couldn't think like that.

"Well, you did a great job. Do you need help with the cleanup?"

"No." Her tone was a little sharp. "I mean, I told you I'd do it."

"Okay. I just thought that two work quicker than one."

She busied herself gathering up the paint supplies. "Is everything okay?" he asked.

"Fine," she said. "I'll have this done in a bit."

"Listen," he said. Moving to stand beside her, he grabbed her hand. "I don't care about the mess."

He did, but he wasn't about to tell her that. He'd hurt

her feelings and hadn't meant to. That was what was important here.

She still didn't look at him. Not good. "Is this about last night? I'm sorry. I had a little too much to drink and…"

"And what? It was a mistake?" Her head lifted and she glared at him. He wasn't sure he'd ever seen her angry like that.

"No. I'd never call it that. Maybe, one of the best nights of my life."

A smile tugged at the corner of her mouth. "One of?"

This time he grinned. "Well, if I tell you it was the best, I'm worried I might scare you off."

"It was good for me, too. And it makes things weird, I get that. But I don't have regrets. Do you?"

"None." *Except now I want to do it all over again. And again.*

"Good. I mean, that's great."

And this was beyond awkward.

"So I saw that you were working on your website and it occurred to me that maybe I could help you with that. I know basic code and a little bit about security."

"You were on my computer?"

He didn't want to say that technically it was his computer.

"My hand bumped the mouse this morning when I was leaving you a note."

"Wait. You left me a note?"

Oh. Ohhhh. She thought he'd left without saying anything. This was all starting to make sense.

"I left the note on the desk."

"I didn't see it."

Huh. "Follow me."

She did. She followed him out the garage door and past the pool. When they made it inside the pool house, he checked where he'd left the note. It wasn't there. Then he knelt down. It wasn't under the desk. He moved the ottoman aside and found the piece of paper.

He handed it to her and she smiled as she read it.

"Am I forgiven?"

"Nothing to forgive," she said. But she held the paper against her chest. She'd thought he'd gone without a word; no wonder she'd been a little sensitive. "Are you serious about helping me with the website? It was supposed to be an easy, do-it-yourself kind of storefront thing, but I couldn't get it to work."

He used the edge of the desk to push himself up off the floor, and then he sat down in her office chair. After reading for a bit, he nodded. "It'll take me a couple of hours, but I should have you up and running tonight."

"Really?"

"Yep. Computers and mechanical stuff are my thing, kind of like design and furniture are yours."

"Oh, it's Friday. You don't have to do it tonight. I'm sure you have plans. Didn't you say you were playing cards or something?"

He had, but that had been when he'd been trying to avoid Chelly. He'd already canceled before heading home from work because he was looking forward to spending more time with her.

"Game was called off. Let me change clothes and I'll order us some pizza. That is, unless you had plans?"

"No, but are you sure? You've been working all day, and I'd hate for you to have to sit and do this."

He didn't mind. "Not a big deal at all." Standing, he went to move past her.

She put a hand on his arm. "Matt?"

"Yes?"

"Thanks for leaving a note, and thank you for helping me."

He couldn't resist; her mouth was doing that pout that just made her so kissable. His lips were on hers and she sighed softly against him. He was about to deepen the kiss, before he remembered she was covered in paint and he was in uniform.

He lifted his head. "Been thinking about doing that all day."

"Me, too," she murmured. "And other things."

His cock hardened. The woman was insatiable. He loved it. "Other things. Yes, those, as well. But if we're going to get your website going, we have to hold off on the other things, because once I get you naked, there will be no stopping. Understood?"

She gave him a sexy smile and a salute. "Yes, sir."

"Nice. I kind of like it when you call me sir." He kissed her quickly and then left. Otherwise he wouldn't have been able to resist her.

Incredible how she already had him wrapped around her little finger.

HE'D LEFT A NOTE.

Damn him. He'd left a note.

All day she'd been mad at herself for being upset that

he left without saying goodbye. That maybe it was his way of saying now they could get back to normal. That they'd scratched their itch and they were friends again, working together on a project.

But he'd left a note.

Chelly,
I have to go, but I still can't stop thinking about you.
–Matt

Here she'd been mean to him in the garage and he couldn't stop thinking about her. Even now he was trying so hard to keep things light. He was joking and she'd been giving him the cold shoulder.

But his expression wouldn't have been able to hurt her if she wasn't so crazy about him. She'd never been so intimate so fast with someone. There had been some great sex in her past, but nothing like the connection she and Matt had.

It was dangerous. Overpowering.

And he wanted to do it all over again.

She was weak. No way would she be able to tell him no. He would respect her wishes if she did, though.

I want him.

Every bit as much as she did last night. Maybe even more now that she knew just how wonderful it could be. As much as she should try to resist, she couldn't.

What a mess. But maybe this is what she needed. A short-term bit of fun to destress. It had been a tough year, and she deserved a little somethin'-somethin'. There were worse things than being wanted by a superhot Marine.

A lot worse things.

Matt returned in board shorts and a tank and gave her a wave before he settled on the office chair, busying himself with what was on the computer. He was determined to help her.

Yeah, she could definitely do worse.

She was due a tall drink of something sexy.

Make mine a Marine, please.

9

WHEN MATT FINISHED the last line of code, he called out for Chelly. She didn't answer. He glanced up at the clock on the computer. It was almost eleven. She'd been popping in every hour or so to see if he needed anything. The last time, she'd used her tank to wipe some sweat off her brow, exposing her belly. He'd almost grabbed her and hauled her into his lap, but she'd kept her distance. After fixing him some tea, she'd disappeared again.

"Chelly?" he called out, searching the nearby garage for her.

She wasn't there, either. Then he heard something scraping against the ceiling.

He headed up to the apartment and paused at the door. She was busy wiping down a table, but it was the rest of the place that made him blink. It was a showstopper. Again, like something he might see in a home and garden magazine. It no longer looked like a storage room. When he was a kid, he used to hide up here as if it was his sanctuary, building forts and pretending to be a soldier or a knight, or sometimes a pirate. It was a great place for make-believe.

But now it looked like a home.

A beautiful one.

"When did you do all of this?"

She jumped and squeaked and then she fell back on the sofa.

He ran to her. "Are you okay?"

She started laughing. So much so she could barely say, "You frightened me."

He had to join in. "Sorry, I was worried when I couldn't find you. This is terrific, but how did you do all of this?"

She shrugged. "One step at a time. We still need to get you a fridge for the kitchen. The one in the main house won't fit up the stairs. I measured. Besides, it would overwhelm the space. And you'll need a new stove. That thing is at least thirty years old. And it's brown. A really ugly brown."

"You did this for me?" He grabbed her and pulled her onto his lap. "Moving this furniture… There was so much of it. You could have hurt yourself."

"I'm stronger than I look."

"I love this. I can't believe you turned this dusty old room into a home. And you did it for me?" he asked again.

"Yes," she said, kissing him lightly. "You've been so good to me. Giving me a place to live and feeding me the last week. I wanted to show you I was grateful."

His brows drew together. She didn't sleep with him because she thought she had to, did she?

"Uh..."

"What?" She gave him a funny look and then her eyebrows popped up. "No, that was... What happened last night, I wanted that. Just as much as you did."

"Whew," he said. "I don't want you to ever feel like I'd take advantage of you, especially like that."

He felt dumb. He'd nearly accused her of having sex with him for a place to stay.

She started laughing again. "Nope. That was two adults who mutually consented to have sex. Hot. Hot. Sex." Then she wiggled on top of him, her movements making him grow harder. "Maybe you should show me *your* gratitude for fixing this place up?" She shifted, fitting him beneath her just right.

"I won't argue," he said.

She paused and then continued laughing. "I'm gross and dirty. And we are not doing anything until I take a shower."

"We could both take one here," he challenged.

"It's not quite big enough for two. Hmmm. I have a better idea." Then she was off him and sprinting for the stairs.

By the time he caught up to her in the backyard, she was at the edge of the pool, taking off her top and bottoms.

All Matt could do was stand there and stare. They had complete privacy and the moon was the only light shining down.

She was gorgeous. From that wild hair falling around her shoulders, to her painted blue toenails. Peaks and valleys—a body a man could spend eternity getting to know.

After pointing at him and saying, "Strip," she dove into the water.

Matt didn't need to be told twice. He quickly yanked off his shorts. Making sure the foil packet he'd put in the pocket was conveniently available by the pool steps.

She swam a few laps and then, when she came up for air, he pulled her to him, their naked bodies melding into one another. He craved her kisses and how she gave herself over so freely.

His hands moved over her slick body, needing to feel as much of her as possible. Her arms wrapped around his neck and then her legs around his waist. The softness of her heat rubbing against his cock was almost more than he could take.

She gasped. He loved the way she responded to his touch and the sweet moans she made when she climaxed. Never would he ever get enough of that sound.

"Matt," she cried, bowing back from him. He kissed her deeply, his hands now caressing her breasts. She moaned again, louder this time.

He had to be inside her. He moved toward the stairs where he'd left the condom, and she clung to him. He sat her on the third step while he tried to put a condom on. But it wasn't easy with wet hands. She rose out of the water like a sea nymph and claimed the protection from him.

"You're taking too long," she said. But before she rolled the condom on him, she slipped his cock into her mouth.

His brain went blank from the sheer pleasure of it. She glanced up at him as she continued to suck him, while stroking the rest of him.

His belly clenched with need; there was no doubt that this nymph held all the power.

"Can't take much more," he muttered, and she stopped. Then she found the condom and slid it on.

He sat down on the step and tugged her on top of him. Her back to his front. It was the only way he could think to save her skin from the hard concrete. "Ride me, Chelly."

She turned and smiled at him and locked her feet behind his knees. She rose and moved smoothly over and then down his erection. And up and down again. And again. And again. They had to fight against the buoyancy of the water, but the angle of her body was perfect for him to reach around and tease her nipples. She increased the tempo.

"That's right, babe. It feels good. You're so incredible. I love watching you just like this."

Her grip on his thighs tightened.

"Oh, Matt, it's too much. I feel…I feel…make me come now," she urged. "Please."

So, so sexy. He teased her, yet at the same time had to hold himself together. He was so close.

"Yes!" she cried out.

"Chelly," he said, his release coming so hard, so intense, it felt like a charging storm. Never in his life had it been like this for him. Ever.

She slowed, lifted off him and then faced him with her legs crossed behind him.

"That was…wow."

"Definitely wow." He could barely speak.

She kissed him thoroughly. This woman was amazing.

Tugging on his ear, she smiled warmly as he looked at her.

"What?"

"I'm hungry."

He laughed. "I forgot to order the pizza, and you've been working really hard all night."

"I know. So you should feed me," she said. "Because I'm not even sure I'm going to be able to walk after that."

He stood up, her legs still wrapped around him. He didn't care if she ever moved. He walked them up and out of the pool. "My room or yours?"

"Your bed is bigger," she said.

"Ah, brilliant and beautiful."

"Yes, sir." She nuzzled his ear. He was definitely beginning to like that. As he carried her inside, she said, "You're strong. Like superhero kind of strong."

"Ha. Wait until you see the rest of my superpowers," he joked.

"There's more? I'd say what we've already done was pretty super. I'm not sure I can take much more."

He shook his head. "Oh, there's so much more." He climbed the stairs with her still in his arms; it wasn't like she weighed much. In the bathroom, he dried her off. "First we get you warm, and then I feed you. You're going to need your strength for what I have planned."

Her eyebrows rose. "Oh, really?"

"Yep." He pointed her toward his bed. She looked very good there, he thought as he pulled the covers up to her chin. "Rest for a bit. I'll be back in a minute with some food."

"Hey, Matt."

"Yeah?"

"Those comic book guys have nothing on you," she yawned. "You're out of this world."

"Right back at you, babe. Get some rest. Like I said, you're going to need it."

"Promises, promises," she said. Yawning again.

He laughed. She'd probably be asleep before he made it to the stairs.

It was midnight, so too late for a pizza run. He sliced up some cheeses and found the grapes she liked. After putting everything on a plate, he grabbed a couple of bottles of water.

He still hadn't shown her the website. He hoped she'd like what he'd done.

When he made it back to the bedroom, she was sound asleep on his side of the bed. He didn't even care.

He was going to need superpowers. Ones that could help make this free-spirited woman understand they belonged together.

Yep. He had it bad.

He was thinking about forever with the one woman who had absolutely no desire for that sort of thing.

A tightrope. That was what he'd be walking. But maybe he could show her how right they were for each other. Make her think all of this was her idea. That putting down roots wouldn't be such a bad thing.

Controlling? Wouldn't that make him just like his father? He felt like he'd been keeping that at bay where she was concerned. Maybe not…

She did want to start a business, and this was as good a place as any to do that.

There was time, he reminded himself. She had to finish the house, which would take…a month? And then there was the river house. He hadn't lied about loving her sketches. She really did get him in a way that most people never did.

Maybe she could grow to care for him. Maybe if they did more things together, she'd want to stay.

He hoped so.

He sounded like some lovesick jerk.

But he couldn't help it.

Because he was having a really tough time thinking about a future without her in it. How quickly she'd become such a big part of him—of his life. He looked forward to coming home from work now, just so he could see her.

And she was so kind. She'd been right about his not wanting to live with the mess during the renovations. He would have been absolutely miserable. She'd gone to the trouble of setting up the apartment for him. That wasn't strictly about her doing a good job. That showed she cared.

He wasn't sure where all of this was going, or how he

truly felt. He had to be with her, though. They needed time to sort things out.

Time. They just needed time.

10

THE NEXT MORNING Matt woke with a start. He was usually up at four, his body on a timer, even if he and Chelly hadn't gone to bed until two. He wasn't surprised to see it was his regular time. Sleep wasn't something he was able to do very well. Maybe it was all the years in the military, but if he woke up during the night, he was staying up.

He turned to check on Chelly.

But she was gone.

He threw on some shorts and went downstairs to see if maybe she was in the kitchen. She wasn't. A trek out to the pool house and he found her on the daybed in a fetal position, hugging a pillow. She was sound asleep.

Strange. He thought she'd stay with him.

He checked his watch; it was a little after four. He put a blanket over her and then shut the door quietly.

The guys would be over at nine to help with the heavy lifting, but he wanted to get the rest of the antiques and extra furniture out of the house before they arrived. He moved the trailer to the front and started carrying out the boxes she'd packed.

When his buddies turned up, he'd already made two trips to the storage facility. She'd done a ton of work he hadn't even realized.

"Where's this amazing woman we keep hearing about?" Ben asked. He, Brody and Marcus, another friend of theirs, had shown up to help.

It was their code. You were always there to help your brothers out.

He wasn't sure where Chelly was. When he'd come back from his last trip, she'd disappeared. He thought maybe she'd be here to at least direct them. And she hadn't left a note.

"She's busy."

"Hey, guys," Chelly said as she came through the open sliding glass doors. "I went and got you all coffee and breakfast sandwiches." Her hair was up in a ponytail, and she had on her cute shorts and a purple top.

She was the most beautiful thing he'd ever seen.

Ben obviously thought so because his jaw had gone slack. Dude was about to lose that jaw if he didn't get his eyes off his girl.

His girl?

"I'm guessing you're Chelly?" Brody asked.

"I am, unless he's hiding some other woman in here that I don't know about," she joked. But the smile didn't seem as wide as it usually was. She had to know he wasn't interested in anyone else.

"Nice to meet you," Brody said and held out his hand. Ben and Marcus lined up to do the same.

They introduced themselves and then, being Marines, they dug into the food.

"Mari tells me you've got a good eye for design," Brody said between chews.

She blushed. He liked her modesty. "Your fiancée's really sweet. How is she?"

Brody rolled his eyes. "She's in full-on controlled chaos mode trying to get the party set up for this afternoon. She wants everything to be perfect for the CO. Please don't tell her I said the chaos bit. Makes her mad. But I was grateful my man here needed a hand moving that stuff. Got me out of the CO's house, at least for a few hours. I did promise I'd be back in time to help her arrange the buffet, so we better get this show on the road."

Chelly put her hands on her hips and looked around. "I thought I'd move some of the smaller boxes, but it looks like those are already gone."

"Thought I'd get a head start," Matt said. "That way the guys just had to help with the larger pieces."

"Always thinking ahead," Ben said. "And saving his buddies work. And sometimes our asses at work."

They all laughed.

WORKING WELL AS a team, they had everything loaded in the trailer in no time. Traffic, however, was being less cooperative.

After a quick lunch that Matt paid for, they completed their last trip to the storage facility. He hadn't seen Chelly on their previous trip. He checked the pool house and the apartment but she wasn't in either location.

He returned the trailer to the rental agency, and when he pulled in at the main house he noticed her truck was gone.

It made him nervous. They were supposed to leave in an hour for the CO's party.

Maybe she was just running an errand? But when she wasn't back once he was out of the shower, he texted her.

She didn't text back.

Was she in trouble? He was about to head out to the pool house to see if her stuff was still there.

Had she left for good?

She wouldn't. Would she?

The garage door opened and she rushed through, almost bumping into him.

"Hey," she exclaimed, stopping short. "Did you guys finish already?"

"We did. But you and I need to leave in a half hour for the party."

She frowned. "That doesn't give me long to get ready. It's later than I thought."

"Where have you been?" His tone sounded so accusatory. "Sorry. That didn't come out the right way. I was just worried about you. I hadn't realized you'd left."

She watched him carefully, as if she was afraid he might do something. Then he remembered. The ex—that's when she'd left him.

"Sorry," he repeated, meaning it. "I really was just worried about you." He took a step back to give her some space.

"That's okay. I sold the two end tables I was telling

FREE Merchandise is 'in the Cards' for you!

Dear Reader,

We're giving away FREE MERCHANDISE!

Seriously, we'd like to reward you for reading this novel by giving you **FREE MERCHANDISE** worth over **$20** retail. And no purchase is necessary!

You see the Jack of Hearts sticker above? Paste that sticker in the box on the Free Merchandise Voucher inside. Return the Voucher promptly...and we'll send you valuable Free Merchandise!

Thanks again for reading one of our novels—and enjoy your Free Merchandise with our compliments!

Pam Powers

Pam Powers

P.S. Look inside to see what Free Merchandise is **"in the cards"** for you!

We'd like to send you two free books like the one you are enjoying now. Your two books have a combined price of over $10 retail, but they are yours to keep absolutely FREE! We'll even send you 2 wonderful surprise gifts. You can't lose!

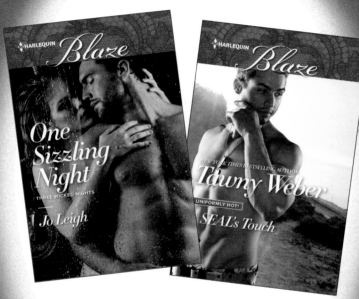

REMEMBER: Your Free Merchandise, consisting of **2 Free Books** and **2 Free Gifts**, is worth over $20 retail! No purchase is necessary, so please send for your Free Merchandise today.

YOUR FREE MERCHANDISE INCLUDES...
2 FREE Books **AND** 2 FREE Mystery Gifts

FREE MERCHANDISE VOUCHER

2 FREE BOOKS and **2 FREE GIFTS**

Please send my Free Merchandise, consisting of
2 Free Books and **2 Free Mystery Gifts**.
I understand that I am under no obligation to buy
anything, as explained on the back of this card.

150/350 HDL GKAV

Please Print

FIRST NAME

LAST NAME

ADDRESS

APT.#

CITY

STATE/PROV.

ZIP/POSTAL CODE

Offer limited to one per household and not applicable to series that subscriber is currently receiving.
Your Privacy—The Reader Service is committed to protecting your privacy. Our Privacy Policy is available online at www.ReaderService.com or upon request from the Reader Service. We make a portion of our mailing list available to reputable third parties that offer products we believe may interest you. If you prefer that we not exchange your name with third parties, or if you wish to clarify or modify your communication preferences, please visit us at www.ReaderService.com/consumerschoice or write to us at Reader Service Preference Service, P.O. Box 9062, Buffalo, NY 14240-9062. Include your complete name and address.

NO PURCHASE NECESSARY!

HB-516-FMH16

▲ Detach card and mail today. No stamp needed. ▶

© 2015 HARLEQUIN ENTERPRISES LIMITED. ● and ™ are trademarks owned and used by the trademark owner and/or its licensee. Printed in the U.S.A.

you about the other day. The ones I painted turquoise. I just dropped them off. The guy bought them as a surprise for his wife. She'd seen my ad online and loved them. Why are you looking at me like that?"

"You went to some stranger's house by yourself?"

Her mouth went to a straight line. "Yes. And I sold the end tables. What is wrong with you?"

Wrong with him? What was wrong with her?

"That guy could have been a serial killer," he said, barely keeping his temper in check. She'd put herself in danger and didn't even seem to care. Not to mention the fact that she was hauling around pieces of heavy furniture by herself. She could have been hurt.

"Yes, because serial killers are well-known for buying bright turquoise end tables for their *wives*. Why are you making this a thing? And why are you acting like some overprotective gorilla? For the record, I've survived fine on my own for a really long time. Years and years. I don't need some protector."

It was when he was about to bring up the past few months of her life, and how she hadn't always made the wisest choices when it came to people, that he stopped himself.

Talk about rubbing it in. She was right; what was wrong with him?

"I was concerned. I thought—"

"You thought what?"

"That you'd moved out." There, he said it.

She looked confused and hurt, as if he'd wounded her. "Why would you think that?"

"You didn't answer the text. Your truck was gone and I couldn't find you."

She sighed. "I was so excited when he called that I left the phone on my desk. I didn't see your text. But why would you automatically think that I'd just up and leave?"

What was he supposed to say? He had to tell her the truth. "You told me you run when things get tough. This job is a big deal, and you've been working so hard. Too hard. And today your smile didn't reach your eyes when you were talking with the guys. You seemed uncomfortable, like you couldn't wait to get out of there."

"They're your close friends, so of course I was nervous. I wanted them to like me. Also, they're huge. I mean, you don't notice because you're their size. But it was like walking into a room full of bodybuilders. Not to mention, I hadn't changed clothes and was a mess. I thought I'd just leave the food on the counter and then you guys were all there. And I was embarrassed, okay? It wasn't how I wanted to look the first time I saw your friends."

"What are you talking about? You're stunning. I was about to punch Ben in the face for looking at you a little too long."

She rolled her eyes. "I guess that's sweet, but let's be clear. You hired me to do a job, so no matter what's going on with this," she said, pointing to him and then to herself, "I'm here until I finish the job. You might think I'm some major flake, but not when it comes to work. That's one thing I take seriously. I have a really great work ethic. I have gone above and beyond for you because I wanted to please you. And this is how you respond?"

She had him there. "You're right. I'm overreacting. It was nuts of me to jump to conclusions. This is new to me. These feelings I have for you. Still, that's no excuse for how I acted."

She dug in her pockets and pulled out a wad of cash. "It's not. I sold the tables for six hundred. Here's your portion. I'm keeping track of every transaction and giving them receipts for the sales so everything can be counted for tax time." She handed over the money.

"Those ugly tables went for six hundred dollars?"

"A piece," she said. "Like I said, that's your part."

"I… You have to be kidding me. This is a joke, right?"

She sighed. "Remember? That's why you hired me. So in the future, I'd really appreciate it if you didn't question me. And if you didn't think I was running off to Alaska or somewhere every time I left the house. It's—annoying."

"I screwed up. I told you that I can be protective. Maybe it's overprotective."

"Definitely. Could be this wasn't such a good idea, mixing business and… Might be best if we stick to business only."

The exact opposite of what he was trying to accomplish here. "Sorry isn't going to cut it, is it?"

"Actually, I'm tired. My head hurts and I hate to bail at the last minute, but I don't feel like going to the party now."

He almost asked if she really had a headache, but that didn't seem the smartest course of action.

"Of course. Have you eaten today? I've noticed that sometimes you forget. That might be why you don't feel well." He shut his mouth tight. Now he was telling her what to do. He had to stop. But he cared about her.

She'd started to walk past him. "Uh. No. It's okay, though, I'm not hungry. I'd rather lie down. You go to the party. Mari will be disappointed if you don't, and you can make excuses for me. Tell her whatever you want."

Then she left him there.

No. He wasn't about to leave her alone if she wasn't feeling well.

He pulled out his phone and texted Brody and Mari.

I messed up bad. We aren't going to make it.

Mari sent a frowny face.
Brody texted him privately.

Do whatever it takes to make it up to her. And maybe stop messing up. Women don't seem to like that in a man.

He typed back Word.

He glanced toward the pool house. Yep. There were some things more important than bonding with his buddies.

After locating some aspirin in the upstairs bathroom, he headed out to the garage. That's where they'd stored the newer kitchen appliances he'd bought. That gave him an idea. He went back to the house and made Chelly a peanut butter and jelly sandwich. And he grabbed a bottle of water from the fridge. He also picked up an apple and put it on the plate.

Knocking lightly with his foot, he waited. But she didn't answer. When he entered she was asleep in the fetal position, hugging the pillow again. Her cheeks were flushed, and he was worried maybe she really was sick. But it was also hot in the pool house. After leaving the plate of food and water on the desk, he scribbled her a quick note. This was becoming a habit. But sometimes it was easier for him to write the words than to say them.

He seemed to have serious foot-in-mouth issues when it came to her. Which was funny, since she said she had the same problem around him.

He didn't want to act all overprotective of her; that was the last thing she needed or wanted. But when it came to her, he wasn't so sure he could keep those instincts in check.

After placing the note next to the plate, he stepped out of the pool house. First, he'd visit the hardware store. He needed supplies.

Yep, time to put his plan in motion.

_11_

WHEN CHELLY WOKE UP, the pool house was pitch-black, and her head was worse than when she'd lain down.

Probably should have eaten something.

She blinked a few times and then yawned. She stretched. Finding something for her head was the first order of business. Then she'd deal with the catastrophe that was Matt.

She turned on the lamp on the nightstand and blinked a few times. That was when she saw the food, the note and more importantly the bottle of pills. She stood, a bit wobbly at first.

Knowing the pills would sit better on a full stomach, she ate the PB&J he'd made her. The man was sweet, she had to give him that. A bit too shielding and bossy, traits she wasn't thrilled about, but so sweet. She chugged some of the water and took a couple of the pills. Then she sat down and read his note.

Beautiful Chelly,
I hope you can forgive me. Of course you can

take care of yourself. You're a strong, independent woman. It's not an excuse, but I find myself feeling very protective of you. But that's my problem, not yours. I'm working on it.

I skipped the party. Didn't seem right going without you. How fun would it be without my favorite person? I'd like to make everything up to you. Come find me when you're feeling better.

–Matt.

How was she supposed to stay mad after that? Like, the sweetest letter ever. And his fault was that he cared too much about her? How ridiculous was that?

Was it weird that they'd known each other such a short time, but they were protective of one another? She'd never had this kind of affinity with a man, and she wasn't sure how to handle it.

In the past, the men she dated always started out nice, but then the criticism would begin. The demands would follow. She could never quite fit into the mold. Their expectations for each other always nose-dived. Quickly.

But Matt was aware of what he'd done wrong; wasn't that half the battle? Who would expect such a tough, no-nonsense guy to be so self-aware and caring? The man had shown her nothing but kindness.

She hadn't been feeling great. And darn if he hadn't pegged exactly what was wrong with her. She had the hangry going on for sure. Hungry and angry were never a good mix.

She took a shower and washed her hair, which helped her head immensely. Feeling a bit better she ventured out. He wasn't in the house, so she headed to the apartment to see if he was there.

The little dining room table was set with a tablecloth, plates and even candles, albeit they weren't lit. That was a good thing since Matt was sound asleep on the couch. He'd hooked up his television and the baseball game was going on. But his eyes were closed and he was on his back.

She couldn't help but smile.

Yeah. How could she stay mad at that handsome man? He really was a work of art. Never in her life had she'd seen a better guy. And he'd done nothing but make her life easier.

He had faults, but who was perfect? Not her, that was for sure.

She took off her flip-flops and tiptoed into the kitchen. There were bags from his favorite hamburger place on the counter. Poor guy, he must have been waiting for her to get up. But she'd slept almost four hours.

The week really had taken it out of her. He was probably right about her trying to do too much at once. It's just that he believed in her, and she so wanted to please him, and not just in bed.

She grabbed the plates from the table and put food on them. He'd bought a fridge and a stove and hooked everything up. How had he gotten those things up the stairs by himself? Then she glanced at him. Those defining muscles of his. So strong.

He'd also brought the good microwave from the main house. She popped the burgers and fries into it and started heating up the food.

When the microwave dinged, Matt sat straight up, his head turning back and forth like he was watching a tennis match, instantly alert.

Marine training, she was sure.

"Hey," he said when he saw her. "How are you feeling?"

"Better, thanks. I'm guessing this is our dinner?"

He nodded. "Sorry, I dozed off. Been a long day."

"I'd say. You moved half a house and then cleaned up this place even more and installed a fridge and stove by yourself."

"Not that big of a deal. You look pretty."

She smiled. Disarming, that one. A little tingle started in her core. Not yet.

"Thanks. Why didn't you go to the party? You didn't have to do all of this."

"I did. I needed to apologize."

"It isn't necessary. The PB&J kind of said it all. And the aspirin. Thanks for that, too."

"You're welcome. I'm new to this. I know I keep saying that. But I'm trying. My relationships in the past— I was always moving around the world. The one time I tried to do something long-term, well, she said she couldn't wait, or rather didn't want to wait around for me to get back from my tour."

"You never told me that. Who wouldn't wait for you? You're awesome."

"Not always. I am sorry."

"These feelings are new to me, too," she said honestly. "But I need you to believe in me, Matt."

"I do, really. You're so talented. I think it was more how you acted around my friends earlier."

"I explained that to you. I was overwhelmed."

"It was more than that," he said, moving closer.

"Well, to be honest, they were all looking at me like I was some kind of alien."

He chuckled. "It's because they've never met anyone I've dated. Ever."

"Ever? But they're your best friends."

"I haven't known Brody that long. But Ben and Marcus, well, I've never been serious enough about a woman to bring her to any of the work functions. And when we all go out, we just party and have fun. This is not where I wanted this conversation to go."

"But you're serious about me?" That was frightening and exciting all at the same time.

"Yes. That's why I keep saying it's new." He held up a hand. "I've never been the jealous type, but you bring it out in me. Not your problem. Like I said in the note. It's something I'm going to have to work on."

She grinned. "You're kind of hot for a Neanderthal."

"I am?" He smiled and moved even closer.

"As long as you don't try to drag me off to your cave, we'll be okay. But you have to let me be me. Trust me."

He stopped. "I do. Trust you. But it's not something I'm really good at. Trusting people, except when it comes to the people on my team. So this might be a work in progress."

"That's exactly what I am, so I absolutely get it."

His arms wrapped around her.

"Maybe you should kiss me," she said. "And then let's commence with the make-up sex."

He laughed. "Nope, not until you eat something else. I'm worried you're working too hard. I realized how much you've done, getting the house ready for renovations. And—"

"And about that overprotective thing?"

He shook his head. "Work in progress."

"I should be grateful that you noticed how much work I've done. This isn't all on you. So we eat, and then we start on the make-up sex. I have a feeling it's going to be epic," she said.

"Epic?" He laughed again. "No pressure or anything."

She put a hand on his cock and squeezed. "You're a Marine. Aren't you guys always up for a challenge?"

"When it comes to you? Always. Oh, I almost forgot."

He ran into the bedroom and then came out with a vase full of summer flowers.

"These are lovely. You didn't have to get me flowers."

"I had them soaking in the bathroom shower. The lady at the florist's said the humidity would help the blooms." He was so serious. She bit the inside of her mouth to keep from giggling.

No one had ever given her flowers. Well, except maybe a corsage for homecoming, but nothing like this.

"Thank you, it's a very sweet gesture."

"There are also chocolates in the fridge. It was so warm in here before I turned the air on and I was afraid they might melt."

"Flowers and chocolate."

"I also tried to find a card but there weren't any that said, *I'm an idiot, please forgive me*."

"I do," she said, as she sat the vase of flowers on the counter. "Forgive you." She touched a few petals and then looked up at him. "But I really think you should kiss me again."

"Whatever you want, babe. Tonight it's all about you."

"Hmm. I feel so powerful. You're going to have your work cut out for you."

"Good thing I got that nap in."

"Yes, yes, it is." And then she kissed him, trying to put everything she was feeling into that kiss.

In the back of her mind there was the tiny worry that she was the first woman he'd been serious about since his ex. That she was the first to meet his friends. And that he felt so strongly about her.

But then he kissed her back and all of her worries disappeared.

This man. He *was* danger packed in a hot body.

But she couldn't quit him.

Not yet.

12

TWO WEEKS LATER they'd settled into a routine. Chelly ended up in his bed most nights. She wouldn't let him into the main house, saying she wanted the renovations to be a surprise. The two times he'd tried to sneak a peek, she'd caught him. And the punishment...

Had been mind-blowing.

She'd teased his cock for an hour before climbing onto him and sending him to paradise.

He couldn't get enough of her or her body. But she was always busy. Between her online storefront and the house, they barely had a few hours together each day. It was never enough.

But it was Saturday, and as soon as she finished going over a few things with the contractor, he and Chelly were heading out to the river house. He couldn't wait to show her the property. It was wrong to be prideful about things, but he'd saved for years to buy the acreage with this special view. It wasn't until about six months after his parents' deaths that he decided to start building his dream house on the property.

Their deaths reminded him, as if he needed reminding, that life was precious and sometimes short.

"Hey." She was flushed again as she came into his bedroom. He'd just gotten out of the shower and was still in his towel. "Oh. Wow. You should just wear towels all the time. You are one extraordinary man."

"Let me demonstrate how extraordinary I can be." He reached for her and pulled her to him.

She batted at his chest, but not very hard. "No time for that. We've got to get out to your property. The contractor is waiting for us."

"I think there should always be time for that."

She slipped her arms around his neck. "Later. I promise. I'll make it up to you."

Then she ripped the towel from his waist and rushed off. "You're a bad, bad girl. I might have to punish you later," he said to her retreating figure. She tossed the towel at him.

"I can't wait. I'll see you downstairs. I have a feeling if I stay up here, we'll miss that appointment."

She had a point. She wore a yellow sundress with brown flip-flops. And all he wanted to do was rip the dress off her body and make love to her. *Focus, Marine. Focus.*

He dressed quickly.

Thirty minutes later they were out at the property. The framing had gone up since the last time he'd been there.

He sat and stared. His house was taking shape.

"Is everything okay?"

Glancing over, he caught her watching him.

"I didn't realize they'd done so much."

Chelly leaned over and kissed his cheek. "I'm trying to get everything finished with an accelerated timetable for you. I have a feeling once we put your parents' house on the market it's going to move fast, especially with the comps I've seen in the area. None of which are going to be as polished, but they're still going for the full asking price within weeks of being listed. So you'll need your house ready. I figure we have two and a half months tops. Cal says he's pretty sure they can get it done, though maybe not all the interior finishes. But we are shooting for completion in late August."

His house. Was he crazy to think about asking her to move into it with him? It was tough moving slowly. Every day he just wanted her more and more. All that emotion and back and forth Brody had gone through with Mari was starting to make sense. His friend had been through hell, but in the end he and Mari managed it. And in a few months they'd be married.

It might be crazy because Brody and Mari hadn't known each other nearly long enough, but he was thinking the same sort of thing about himself and Chelly. He couldn't tell her. She was like a deer in the headlights if they ventured into relationship talk.

Not that he was one for talking about feelings. So he tried to show her every night how much he cared for her. Like taking care of the little things. And every couple of days he'd bring her a little surprise. Just something small.

And she'd done the same for him. She'd given him a tiny replica of his dream house to show him what she was creating for him.

It was one of the most touching gifts he'd ever received.

"Cal's waiting for us," she said.

They went through the structure with the contractor, talking about the best places for outlets, windows and door placement. There wouldn't be many doors, as the main space was open. The living area, kitchen and dining room were all one big area, with a glass wall looking out to the river. There was a hallway leading toward the master bedroom on the right, which had another wall of windows. The bathroom would have more privacy, but there would be a shade that could rise so he'd be able to sit in the bath or take a shower and look out on the water. Then there were two guest rooms on the other side of the kitchen down a small hallway with a guest bath.

His dad would have loved this place. The one thing they did have in common was fishing. His dad had always talked about how he'd be happiest living in a shack by the side of a river.

This was far from a shack, but he'd be able to walk out his back door and go fishing anytime he wanted.

Matt walked out to the cliff and looked down at the river. It was a little low, but it always was in the summer. The whole house was lifted about twelve feet off the ground. He'd have plenty of storage under it, but if the river did flood, he'd have some extra protection.

Arms wrapped around him from behind. He squeezed her hands and then turned to face her.

"Your place is to die for," she said. "It's going to be an amazing sanctuary for you."

For us, he wanted to say. "Thanks. My parents helped me pick it out."

"They did?"

"When I was on tour, they'd go and hunt down properties. They'd send me pics. One time I was laid up a bit, and I was going through emails from Mom. She and Dad had taken a ton of pictures of this place. It just… I knew when I saw this view. It was fall and the trees were changing color. We don't get a lot of that here, we're a little far south for fall color, but the trees were gold and red."

"Then there's the fishing right outside your back door," she said.

"You know me well." He laughed and playfully squeezed her hand. "The pictures of this place got me through some really tough times. It's funny that you called it a sanctuary. I always kind of think of it that way."

"So I was talking to Cal about your barn. It's almost as big in square footage as the house. What are you going to put in there?"

"I wanted a place to keep a boat and trailer. And I like working with my hands. I thought I might set up a woodworking shop or something."

"You are very good with your hands."

"Is that so?"

"Very so," she said. "By the way, I have another surprise for you.

"You do?"

"Yep, come back to the house."

"Where's Cal?" he asked as he put an arm around her shoulders. He liked sharing his place with her.

"He's gone. Had another meeting to get to." They climbed up the back steps—cinder blocks that had been erected to temporarily get in and out of the house. Eventually, there would be a wood deck that wrapped all the way around the house.

In the middle of the family area, she'd set up a blanket and a picnic basket.

"Where did you hide all of this?"

She waggled her eyebrows. "It's magic. Actually, I put it all in Cal's truck ahead of time and told him if he touched the food, he'd regret it."

"Wow. No wonder the construction guys are scared of you."

She rolled her eyes. "I just know what I like, and when it comes to my work, I expect perfection."

"I think you made the carpenter cry the other day."

"You're so mean. I did not make him cry. But it's not my fault he had the wrong moldings on the cabinet doors. And trust me, if you'd seen them, you would have agreed with me." She sat down on the blanket and he did the same.

"Who knew my sweet little Chelly was such a taskmaster?"

"You should have known. I'm pretty darn good at bossing you around."

"True that, love. True that."

She'd been pulling sandwiches out of the little basket, but she paused.

Hold it. What had he said? Love?

"I thought we could watch the sunset," she said. She handed him a bottle of wine. "You open this." She then passed over a corkscrew.

He did the honors, watching her carefully to see if his words had bothered her.

"I'm fine. It's a nickname, right? You call me love, and I call you Neanderthal."

No. "Yes, exactly like that. What kind of sandwiches are those?"

"I scored some of those chicken salad ones from that bakery you like. She also had your favorite éclairs. I may have bought a few more than necessary of those."

He popped the cork and poured wine into the glasses she'd brought.

After they fixed their plates, she held up her glass. "To beautiful new homes and lovely sunsets."

"And gorgeous women," he added. "Well, one gorgeous woman."

"Good save."

"Eat fast. I want to make love to you in my house."

She coughed and he patted her on the back. "Here? Out in the open? What if someone from the river sees us?"

"We're up pretty high and set back. They won't see us. Besides, you promised to make it up to me tonight, and it's almost tonight."

She grinned. "You know, it's really hard to tell you no."

"I know, love." He leaned over and kissed her, and then he whispered in her ear, "Wait until you see what I can do with that éclair."

13

Since their return from the river house, he and Chelly had been in his bed in the garage apartment. He'd dozed off a bit, but now he felt her shift. She was getting ready to leave his bed. Reaching out, he put a hand around her waist.

"For once. Stay," Matt said. "I want you here when I wake up."

She bit her lip.

"Talk to me, Chel. Come on."

"I just like sleeping alone."

In a fetal position while hugging a pillow. It's how he'd found her almost every morning.

"Is it me? Do I snore? Or hog the bed?"

She nodded. "Yes to both of those, but that doesn't really bug me that much."

"So what is it?" She started to pull away. "It's just me and you. Things are good, right? Am I wrong to think this thing is good between us? Why do you keep holding back?"

"I hate talking about feelings."

"Well, that's a start. At least you admitted you have some."

Her brows drew together.

"Babe, I'm just messing with you. I'm not pushing. I'm a patient man. I want you with me as much as possible. I care about you, and I hate waking up without you."

"It makes it all too real if I stay. I'm afraid of getting too comfortable. Bad things happen when I get too comfortable."

He shook his head. She must have been through more than she'd admitted to him. "It's okay. You don't have to stay. I told you, I won't push."

"It's just—the way you make love to me like you do. Like I'm it for you. It scares me because I want more. So much more. But I'm worried." She brushed her fingers across his jaw.

"Don't be, and you are it for me. That isn't easy for me to say, I'll be honest. Everything has happened really fast. And I know you've been through a tough time and this is definitely not in the plan for either of us. It's unexpected, but that doesn't mean we shouldn't try. We're good together and it feels right. You here with me. Do you feel the same way?"

She nodded. "But that doesn't make it easier. It makes it harder. I don't have a great track record with relationships. You're a really nice guy. And you deserve someone who is ready for the white picket fence. I'm not there. I'm just getting going with my career. I don't settle easily. I like to keep things easy."

He was ready for that picket fence, as scary as that

might be. But he didn't want it with anyone—he wanted her. "There aren't any fences at the river house. I'm simply asking you to spend the night, Chel. I'm not asking for any kind of commitment. I mean, we practically live in the same house as it is. What's the big deal? You're sleeping a few hours in my bed. I'd sleep in yours, but I don't fit."

She rolled her eyes. "You and I know that means more."

"Just a little more," he said. "How about this, just tonight. Just stay with me tonight. Don't run off to the pool house. We'll take this one day at a time, okay?"

"Okay. Tonight."

He grinned and then kissed her. "Don't sound so happy about it."

"But if I'm staying, you have to do what I say."

"Oh, really?"

"Yep." She gently shoved him flat on his back, and then she climbed on top of him. "Touch me," she said.

"Where?" She wanted to play, and he'd let her.

She picked up his hands and put them on her breasts. "Here."

Then she positioned her softness over his cock and began rocking back and forth. When her hand traveled down his body, he hardened instantly.

So hot, this one.

She grinned and then gasped as she began moving faster and faster. The pressure on his cock was just right and he bucked underneath her. Watching her like this was one of the most erotic things he'd ever seen. The woman could go from zero to sixty in nothing flat.

"Open your eyes," he said. "I want to see them when you come."

She gave a slow smile. "I'm the boss," she whispered and bent to kiss his mouth. He pinched one of her nipples and she moaned. "Yes." Her fingers moved even faster as she watched him.

"You're unbelievable," he said.

And then she came, her body tensing and shaking.

"I need to make love to you, babe. Now."

She guided him into her heat. She was so ready for him. He nearly lost control right there. Had to bite down on his tongue to stop it. Then she put her hands on his biceps and began rocking back and forth again.

Matt met her hurried pace, needing to find his release just as much.

"Again," she said as her muscles tightened around his cock. So responsive.

He gave in to her, pulling her to him so he could taste her honeyed lips. He thrust hard, bringing her with him as he slid over the edge.

And he was over, as in head over heels.

She wasn't the only one who was scared.

THE WAY HE touched her. The way he looked at her.

Chelly knew.

This Marine, well, he was everything. Kind. A good man with a huge heart.

It would be easy to stay in his bed for as long as he would have her. But that was why this could only be temporary.

Because this one was going to hurt worse than all the others combined when it ended. And it would end.

She'd made a promise to sleep in his bed and she would—tonight. But she would need an exit strategy, one that might keep her heart intact if that was even possible.

She curled into his side; his arm was tight around her, almost as if he still expected her to run. Couldn't blame him. She had been running back to her bed every night. A coward, afraid to get too comfortable. She hadn't lied about that. She listened to him breathing. He was asleep.

Something he didn't do much of, she'd noticed. Maybe it was a Marine thing, but he only slept four or five hours a night. And he always seemed to have so much energy. He ate well and took pretty good care of himself. He worked out with weights several times a week, and he went for runs every other day. He said they also did training on the base.

She wasn't much for running, but she had managed to swim daily. It was relaxing. And truthfully, every time she left his bed she swam until she was so tired she fell into an exhausted sleep.

"You okay?" he said, snuggling closer.

"How did you know I was awake? You were sleeping."

"Relaxed, not sleeping. And I'm a Marine—always aware of my surroundings."

"You never talk about it, being a Marine."

"Not a lot to tell."

"Don't believe you," she said. "I noticed the scar

from the bullet hole in your back. And that long, jagged scar on your hip."

"Not much I can tell you. The bullet hole was a sniper in Baghdad. Through and through. I turned just in time, or it would have gone through the heart."

What? "You could have died." She put her hand over his heart. It was horrible to think he might not be here right now.

"Happened first week of my first tour. I was pretty sure I was the worst Marine ever recruited, nearly getting killed my first week." He laughed.

"How can you laugh? Matt, that's awful. *You could have died.*"

"But I didn't. The week after I was sent home, half my platoon was killed by a suicide bomber. That sniper did me a favor."

The sadness in his voice pulled at her heart. He felt guilty because he was alive. That was obvious. "Wow. You're so brave. I don't think I could have gone in the first place, but after being shot, you went back."

"Four more times. It's what we do. I had my job, which was flying those Apaches and making sure the maintenance crews were trained. I'd fly anywhere to save one of my brothers or sisters."

"What happened with your hip? That's a pretty long gash."

"My last tour, we landed in the middle of a firefight. We were trying to get the injured out. One of the med techs went down trying to assist someone else. I had him on my shoulder when I was attacked from out of nowhere with a machete. I turned to protect the guy on my shoulder and the machete came across me. I actually thought he'd done more damage."

"Matt! You're lucky to be alive. What happened?"

"Well, my hands were busy so I did the only thing I could. I kicked the hell out of him. Got my guy on the transport and got out of there ASAP."

"You flew a helicopter with a wound like that?"

"There wasn't anyone else to do it, and I had to get the injured out of there."

"Yeah, but you were injured, too." She sat up and put her hands on either side of his face. A tear slid down her cheek.

"Love," he said and thumbed the tear away. "I was the only one who could get us out of there. It was my job. I lost a lot of blood by the time we made it back to base, but the doc was able to sew me up fast, and I was moving a few hours after surgery."

"Back into the war?"

"No. Not quite that fast. Though if they'd cleared me to fly... We were in Africa, I can't say where, but it was a bad scene. We lost a lot of Marines. And no one here will ever know what happened. And don't cry. It was years ago. On a couple of my tours nothing happened. I'm one of the lucky ones. I made it home alive."

"Still." She sniffed. "I feel like such a brat whining about how tough things have been for me the past year, and you've nearly been killed twice and you lost your parents."

"Hey." He grabbed her wrists. "Your life is just as important as mine. And our experiences are different, but yours are no less significant. I just wish you'd tell

me more about your past. Why it is you feel you have
to run all the time?"

She pursed her lips. "Is this one of those quid pro
quo things?"

He let go of her wrists and brushed the hair from her
cheek. "Only if you want to talk."

"Unlike yours, my experiences are just about making some really bad choices. You know about the jerk
I was dating last year."

"The one who was following you on your phone?"

"Yes. Before the stalker stuff happened, I gave him
money. He said it would be a loan but I was so stupid
to believe him. But my story just sounds like loserville
compared to what you've gone through. That's why—"

How did she make him understand?

"You're being so careful."

She sighed. He did get her, probably better than anyone ever had. Kind of in the same way she understood
him.

"Yes."

"So before you landed in Nashville you were traveling the world. How long?"

"Since…" She blew out a breath. Oh. Crap. That.
She never thought about that. Ever. She didn't want to.

"You don't have to tell me. It's okay."

She took a deep breath. "No, it's fine. It's just that I
never talk about it. My life was really different before
my junior year of college. I wasn't so—I'd never been
Miss Straight and Narrow, but my life was on track.
And then…" Emotion clogged her throat.

He scooted up so he was sitting and then drew her

into his lap. "You don't have to tell me." He stroked her hair.

But she did. She needed to tell someone.

"My brother was two years older than me. He overdosed. He and his friends were on a skiing trip, and things got out of control."

She took another breath. "He was the golden child. The perfect one. The standard to which all other children—meaning me—were held. My parents—they took it hard. They wanted me to take his place or something. It was almost as if they were punishing me because he wasn't there. After the funeral, I couldn't take it. So I took the money I had and I went to Paris, which happens to be even more expensive than New York. But I found a hole to live in with four other design students. I worked three jobs and did internships with different design studios.

"And after that, it was easier to stay on the move than go home and face what was going on there. Mom ended up... She took a few too many pills. Dad flew me home to talk to her, but she was angry with me. Blamed me for basically everything. Said she'd wished I'd been the one who died."

"Babe." Matt squeezed her tight. "She didn't mean it."

"No. She did. She's not a bad person, but my brother was always her favorite. She made no bones about that the whole time we were growing up. Dad was better. I wasn't really a daddy's girl, but he did speak up for me more than once. But then, once Mom said that, he thought it might be best for me to go. That she needed time."

The tears fell now. She missed her mom and dad in spite of everything. She didn't care that they weren't exactly the world's greatest parents; they were her family. "That was four years ago. They've reached out a couple of times, but I just... Maybe it makes me a bad person, but I don't need to be around parents who don't really want me. Not good for the soul, you know? It's taken a lot of reflection, but I think I'm better off not being in that environment. I'm never going to be the perfect daughter they want me to be, and I can't handle their disappointment."

"That's rough, Chel. I'm sorry. I was lucky in the parents department, but when they died... I get it. For you, it's like you lost all of that, but they're still alive. Has to be even worse. My dad was a hard-ass, but I never doubted his love. And he was proud of me. After I came home that first time, he tried to talk me into staying home. Mom was behind most of that. I'm an only child, so... But they understood. I can't imagine what you've gone through."

"That's why I sort of run from being comfortable. It's just easier to keep going, you know? I thought Nashville was going to be my home. That I might put roots down there, but...that didn't go so well."

"We're not all bad guys," he said.

"Yep. I know. You're one of the good ones, but I'm always waiting for the other shoe to drop. It's not right. I get it, but it's how I'm wired."

"So we start slow, like we said. Tonight you sleep in

my arms. And tomorrow, well, we figure it out when it gets here."

"You're awesome. Now and forever."

He kissed her and she wiggled, trying to tease him.

"Keep doing that and you're going to get a whole lot of awesome."

"Promises, promises."

He flipped her onto her back. "That's the second time you've said that. I'm about to show you that I always keep my promises."

There was a smile on his face, but a new intensity in his eyes.

"Show me," she said.

And he did.

14

CHELLY'S PHONE WAS ringing way too loud. Matt had left for work two hours earlier. Since their talk, circumstances had done a one-eighty, and now she couldn't sleep if she *wasn't* next to him. She tried not to think about the implications of that. She picked up the phone. It was Mari. "What's up?"

"You. I need you up and at my office in an hour," Mari said. "I need your help with something. Bring your portfolio and the sketches and anything that shows what you can do. And look professional. But funky, you know."

"Wait. What?"

"One hour. Do *not* be late." Then she hung up.

So much for sleeping in. *Did I just dream that?*

Her phone buzzed again.

Hurry.

It was a text from Mari. Evidently it wasn't a dream. As she ran through the house she could hear the workmen. The main house was really coming along fast. Cal was a miracle worker, and his team so efficient. From the stories she'd heard it wasn't normally this easy with renos, not that they hadn't run into problems, but Cal handled everything so professionally she never had to worry.

After a quick shower in the pool house she dug through her clothes. What was professional but funky? And it was hotter than hot outside. She grabbed a cute black mini, a frilly white gauzy top with beading that was light and cool.

Shoes. She was about to put on the strappy heels she'd worn to dinner the other night with Brody and Mari. They'd done a couples thing. It was fun. So much fun. And weird.

She was a couple. She and Matt. Yes, definitely weird.

After digging in the back of the closet, she found her black cowboy boots. They were her lucky boots. Exactly what she needed for this meeting, whatever it was about.

She gathered up her iPad, her sketchbook and put everything in the leather portfolio Matt had bought her. A considerate gesture, although she had a feeling the portfolio had more to do with the fact that she was always leaving her sketches all over the place. He thought it might help if she had a place to put them. And keep things tidy. She smiled at the image of Matt that burned through her brain.

When she finally hopped into her truck, it was ten minutes to the hour.

Crap. Crap. Crap.

At least the meeting wasn't too far away. When she

pulled up in front of the quaint little house where Mari's design firm was, it was only three minutes past the hour. Abbott was waiting for her on the porch.

"Okay, so as of right now you're an associate of the design firm. We have a very important client visiting. When you see said person, you're going to freak out a little because she's famous. But you have to act like you meet people like that every day. She wants a recording studio designed, and if you do a good job on that, well, you might get to do her mansion."

Abbott was talking so fast, Chelly could barely keep up.

"Why can't Mari do it? Or you?"

"Mari's sick and can't make the meeting. And I'm already stretched thin covering a bunch of clients. And this really isn't my sort of thing. Mari's the closer. I tend to scare people away. But you're charming and funny, just the sort folks like to deal with. I just need you to go in there and impress the heck out of her. Okay? She's very picky. And there's a ninety-nine percent chance she's going to go with someone else, but Mari's freaked out so we have to at least try."

"What's wrong with Mari?"

"Flu," Abbott said. "Can't get out of bed right now."

"In late June?"

"Please, just go in there and be your darling self. Show her some sketches. Answer her questions. Easy peasy, right?"

It didn't make sense why Abbott couldn't do it; she was Mari's partner. But they'd both been really kind to her, so she wouldn't let them down. Or at least she'd try not to.

Abbott shoved her through the front door, through reception and into Mari's office. A woman stood as Chelly entered. "Oh, hi," the woman said.

"Hey." Chelly gave her a little wave. That was Carrie McIntire. She blinked several times. Only one of the most successful country recording artists ever. She was in her late twenties, but she was already a legend in Nashville.

"Sorry I was running a little late," Chelly said.

"It's okay. I just got here." She had a bit of a twang. "Mari says you've got tons of talent. Did she explain what I wanted?"

"Yes, a recording studio."

"That's where I want to start. I know you haven't had time to pull anything together since I called her this morning. I had a show in Dallas last night. We were gonna fly home this morning, but I saw the layout of Mari's house in a magazine spread. And I was like, I got to talk to this girl. But then she said she had the flu, and since I was already here, she said she'd send one of her best."

No pressure or anything.

"Well, thanks for coming in," Chelly said. This was all feeling a bit surreal. This woman's songs had helped her get through her last breakup. Probably wasn't professional to say that.

"You're welcome," Carrie said. At least she was polite.

"Listen, Carrie, I'm going to be honest, I have no idea what I grabbed off my desk for this," Chelly admitted.

"It's okay. Abbott showed me some of their other designs. But they said you kind of have that Nashville flair. I can't find a designer I like there. They all go a little too shabby-chic or too cookie-cutter, you know?"

"Well, a lot of what I do is more repurposing things."

"I like that," said Carrie. "Like making old stuff look new. It's good for the environment. I just don't like everything white and frilly."

"Ah. Okay then." She pulled out some of the sketches she'd done. "This one is a local plantation house I'm redoing. It's not really the kind of style you're going for, but it fits the house."

"I *love* this kitchen. I'd do these cabinets in a grayish-blue, though."

Chelly laughed. "I would, too, but the owner is selling the house. So I had to keep things kind of neutral."

"Got it," Carrie said. "That makes sense."

"Once we're done, I'll add some pops of color with accessories so it feels a bit more homey. They're finishing up the floors today, so we're not quite there yet."

She pulled out pictures of Matt's river house. "This is another project that's in the works. It's more casual."

"Oh, this is it," Carrie said. "Natural and rustic, but fresh. Yes. Yes. I love this. Show me everything."

Chelly did.

The singer was very honest about what she liked and what she didn't.

When they'd finished with the sketches, she showed her some of the photos of the furniture she'd redone. "No way…that TV cabinet used to be that dresser? Wow. Girl, you've got skill."

"Thanks."

"So, I have my studio attached to the house. It's rough right now. It was actually the original log cabin on the property. We need to work with my acoustics guy. I'm tired of traveling back and forth to New York and LA to work with different producers. I've got a big house and everything I love is there. So I want them to come to me. But we got to make this place state of the art. You interested?"

Surreal. This wasn't happening. "Yes."

The singer jumped up. "Great. Why don't you work up some sketches? I'll get my PA to send you the dimensions and stuff, but you should come to Nashville and see the place."

Back to Nashville. Her stomach turned.

"What do you have against Nashville?" Carrie asked. "I can see it on your face."

Dang. The woman was perceptive.

"Nothing," she answered a little too quickly. "I used to live there. My, uh, ex is there." *Shut your mouth. This woman doesn't care about your crazy ex.*

"Nasty piece of work from the look on your face. Don't worry. I have the world's best security team. No one gets on my property."

Chelly had a feeling she wasn't joking.

"I'll put some sketches together and if you like those, we'll get the paperwork going," Chelly said. She had no idea what kind of contracts Mari used, but it was always best to have everything laid out on paper, especially with a celebrity like Carrie.

"Yay. That was worth the stop here, after all. Well, girl. I gotta get going. Oh. You got a pen?"

Chelly grabbed one off Mari's desk and a piece of paper. "This is my number. The one underneath is my assistant's. Half the time she's got my phone, anyway. And this is my email. Can you get me something together by the end of the week? We really need to begin on the space. I gotta cut my new album over the next two or three months or my record company is going to kick my butt."

"Sure." Chelly's head hurt. How was she going to come up with sketches that fast? *And since when do you say no to an opportunity?*

"Girl, this was meant to be. You're going to set Nashville on fire. I just know it."

Then she was gone.

Chelly sat in the chair on the other side of Mari's desk, staring at the wall. The door opened again, but she was too in shock to even look to see who it was.

"What just happened?" she asked.

Abbott sat down across from her. "I think you just nabbed yourself a huge client."

"*We* did it. I would never have met her if it weren't for you and Mari. She wants sketches by Friday. Friday. That's two days away and I haven't seen the space."

"Mari's having the assistant send over a lot of photos for you, and the specs. They're being emailed to you as we speak."

"How did Mari know?"

"I was standing outside in the hall, texting her every

word. Well, as much as I could. That woman talks really fast."

"I can't believe all of this. When I woke up this morning—"

"I can't believe you closed her. Want to know something supercrazy?"

"I'm not sure how much more crazy I can take this morning."

Abbott laughed. "The assistant told Mari that Carrie has interviewed over thirty different designers in the last two months. From Nashville, LA, New York and even some from Paris and London. You were the first one she asked to do sketches. The assistant is calling it a win."

She couldn't wait to tell Matt. He'd be so excited for her.

"Nashville?" Matt asked.

She glanced up at the tone. They were on the couch in the garage apartment. He was watching a baseball game, while she worked on her sketches. She'd just told him the whole story.

"Honestly, I'm not so excited about going back there, but she says she has great security. If I can find a contractor like Cal who doesn't need a lot of managing, I won't have to be there much until it's time to decorate. That is if she likes the sketches, which she might not. She's seen a bunch of different designers. Including a few famous ones. I mean, why would she want my ideas?"

"Of course she'd want your designs." Matt put a hand on her shoulder. "She'd be lucky to have you."

That hard tone was gone and her Marine cheerleader was back in play.

"I'm lucky to have you," she said. "I'm nervous about working for Carrie. I mean, you're my biggest client so far. And you're pretty easy to please."

Even with his compulsion to keep everything neat and organized, he'd still been wonderful.

"But you've been traveling the world, and you're always working on projects and sketching. Mari believes in you. So do I."

"Who knows what might come of it, but I have to try, right?"

"Absolutely," he said. "I'm gonna grab a beer. You want something? A bottle of water?"

"You know what? I'll take a beer. I want to celebrate. But just one, because I really have to work on these sketches."

He headed into the kitchen. "I should keep some champagne on hand for celebrations like this."

"I'm a simple girl. Beer is good enough for me."

He popped the top and handed the can to her and then did the same with his. After taking a long pull, he sat the beer on the coffee table. "Once you turn in your sketches, I'll take you out for a real celebration. Okay?"

He was always so thoughtful. "You don't have to do that, Matt, really. You're so sweet. Telling you about the meeting was the first thing I thought of when Carrie left. Well, that and how was I going to do this."

"You couldn't wait to tell me?" He was still standing and there was an odd look on his face.

"What?"

He reached for her beer and sat it by his on the table. Then he took her hands and pulled her up. His arms wrapped around her.

She needed to work, but then his lips were on hers and she forgot what she was thinking.

An insistent ringing pulled at her consciousness. "Ignore it," he said against her lips.

"Ignored," she said. Only slightly worried it might be Nashville calling.

His lips returned to hers, but then his phone started going off. And then hers was ringing again.

They laughed and pulled apart.

"It's Mari."

"It's Brody."

They both answered.

"This better be good," Matt said. "What? Yes, she's here."

"Mari, what's going on?" Chelly asked. "Are you guys okay?"

"Yes," her friend said. "Brody," she yelled, "hang up. They're together. I'll put her on speaker."

"He hung up," Matt said, waving his phone.

"I've got them on speaker," Chelly said.

"What is going on?"

"We're getting married," Mari and Brody said together.

"Uh, yeah. You're getting married in October. Fall wedding. It's what Mari always wanted," Matt said.

She and Matt looked at each other as if their friends had gone off the deep end.

"No. Saturday. We're getting married Saturday in Houston. And we need you guys there," explained Brody.

"What happened? She's not pregnant, is she?" Matt joked.

Everyone laughed.

"Yes, she is," Mari said. "The doctor confirmed it this morning."

"Oh," Matt said. *"Oh."*

"Yeah. Oh," Brody said. "Still not sure how it happened."

"Dude, we've had the birds and the bees chat. Do I need to go over it again?" Matt teased.

"Funny," Mari said.

"I'm so happy for you both," Chelly gushed. "But why Houston? Everyone you know is here."

"My dad's still doing chemo down there. It'll be his last week. But he can't travel. Not yet. And we want him there."

Chelly choked up. That they would go to all that trouble for his dad. She sniffed.

"Tell us what you need," she managed to get out. Even though she hadn't known Mari and Brody long, she felt quite close to them.

"Nothing except for you to show up," Mari said. "We're keeping it simple. I'm making my bouquet. Brody just bought me a dress. And his dad already found the minister for us. So that leaves our friends. We decided friends, family and maybe some cake. Abbott's working on that. Simple."

"Sounds wonderful. Of course we'll be there for you," Chelly said. "Right, Matt?"

He was smiling so big. "Hell, yes. Just tell us what time and where."

"We'll text you the info. See you soon."

They hung up.

"So not the flu," Chelly said. "I thought it was weird to have that this late in the summer."

"Well, now we know the flu is sometimes code for baby."

"That's why she couldn't make it to the meeting this morning. She was at the doctor."

Ah. The funny look Abbott had given her when she said Mari had the flu.

"Saturday."

"That's really fast."

"Yep," he said.

"We have to get them a gift. And I've got to get these sketches done. And I need to run out to the river house tomorrow. Gotta look at paint colors in the sunlight."

"They have one of those register thingies. It was on their *save the date* invite they sent out last month. If you check online and tell me what I should get, I can handle the gift. I can also drive to the river house and decide on the paint colors."

"I can do the paint colors. But I will definitely take you up on picking up the gift."

"We make a great team," he said.

She glanced up at him. He had the biggest smile on his face.

"Yes, we do. You're really happy for them, aren't you?"

He nodded. "I like it when good things happen to

good people. They are some of the best. They'll make great parents."

That's when it hit her. He wanted what Brody and Mari had.

In fact, if she was honest, she did, too. Someday.

Just not right then.

"They will."

Crap. Crap. In all the crazy, she'd forgotten the most important thing.

Keeping her heart safe.

She glanced up at him, her big tough Marine who was beyond happy for his friends.

Her heart wasn't safe.

It wasn't safe at all.

15

"YOU ARE THE most beautiful bride I've ever seen," Chelly said to Mari, "but if you don't stop squeezing those flowers so hard you're going to break the stems." They were with Mari's sister, mother and Abbott, who was doing some last-minute altering of the dress.

"How could I have gained three pounds in two days?" Mari fretted, her hands shaking slightly.

"You're pregnant," they all said in unison.

"And it's no big deal." Abbott smiled. "I just had to let out an inside seam. Take a deep breath." That had been part of the problem. Mari put the dress on and it buttoned up, but she couldn't breathe. They were worried she might pass out.

The bride took a deep breath, and the whole room seemed to relax with her. "I can't believe you found such a beautiful dress so quickly, one that needed so little fixing," Chelly said.

"It was Brody. After we had everything confirmed by the doctor, he took me home so I could nap. Because

I'd spent the last two weeks thinking I had the flu and a baby hadn't even... Well, that wasn't supposed to happen yet. It was all a bit much and I might have had a tiny breakdown and screamed at him to go away. When I woke up there were presents. A dress and these shoes. He bought me such lovely girly shoes. In the right size."

"I helped," Abbott said. "Might have been my favorite shopping trip ever. That Marine in a bridal store trying to show the owner your shape. And then telling her that you looked like an angel and that he needed a dress that looked like something an angel would wear."

"That might be the most romantic thing I've ever heard." Chelly teared up a little. These big tough guys all seemed to have such a tender side. She had to include Matt in that description. Now it was her turn to take a deep breath.

"And then he said he and his dad found a chapel and that we were getting married because his kid was going to have his name from the get-go and he wasn't taking any chances. Then he showed me the dress, and I could not have picked out a more perfect one."

It was gorgeous from the sweetheart neckline to the covered buttons down the back, to the beautiful beaded lace that shimmered ever so slightly when she moved. "That was all him," Abbott said. "They showed him thirty different dresses, so it wasn't like he picked the first one. He was so serious about it. Cutest thing I've ever seen."

"And now I'm getting married." Mari said that last part on a whisper. "Today."

"Are you having second thoughts?" Chelly shouldn't

have said it, but she also didn't want her friend to feel trapped. "I mean, I know you love him, but you don't have to do anything you don't want to."

Why won't my mouth stay shut?

Everyone turned to stare at her and then Mari started laughing. She waved a hand in front of her face. "Oh, whew. I needed that. I don't feel trapped at all. I can't wait to marry him. He's the best thing that has ever happened to me. It's just happening really fast. But I kind of love that you were ready to grab a getaway car and run if I needed you to."

That's what Chelly did. She ran.

She shrugged. "Just looking out for my friend." And then she winked at her to make it seem like she'd been joking, even though she hadn't.

They left the room by the side of the chapel to enter the chapel proper.

Brody's dad and the CO stood up for the groom. Abbott and Mari's sister were beside the bride. The little chapel had beautiful stain-glass windows, and the colors shone through on the couple as if they were blessed.

They were. While Chelly had never been a fan of weddings, this one tugged at her heart. Maybe because she understood how much love they shared as a couple. Never in her life had she seen a bride and groom more perfect for one another. It was a heartwarming moment.

Matt squeezed her hand as the couple said their I dos. She glanced up to find him fully engaged in what was happening. Was this what he wanted? A trip down the aisle?

She wasn't sure if she could commit to a lifetime of

anything. Even with someone as wonderful as Matt, and she was fairly certain there would be no better man for her.

But trapped with the same guy until death do us part seemed pretty permanent. Chelly wasn't sure she could do permanent.

Her career was taking off, and if she was lucky enough to get the job in Nashville, it might mean a lot of travel. She had a feeling that he wouldn't be thrilled about that.

He was still constantly going over her numbers and double-checking that everything was as she said it was. She didn't blame him, but it sometimes bothered her that he didn't fully trust her to do the job right.

Everyone stood as the couple came down the aisle hand in hand, giant smiles on their faces.

"I'm not sure I've ever seen anyone happier," Matt said.

She nodded.

The rest of the wedding party came down the aisle. Then the minister announced, "The bride and groom, and their families, would like you to meet them at the reception across the street."

Mari had only wanted cake, but her parents went all out and rented an Italian restaurant for the reception. Once they'd crossed the street, Matt took her in his arms outside the restaurant.

"Have I told you how beautiful you are today?" He kissed her cheek.

"Only five or six times. It's okay. I'm sure you'll make it up to me." That was one of the things she adored about him. He always took notice of what she wore, or if she'd tried something different with her hair. In so many ways, especially the ones that counted, he was the perfect man.

He squeezed her tight and nuzzled her ear. "Tell me how I can make it up to you."

She turned her head so her lips were at his ear. "Hot. Sex."

He growled. "Woman, I'm hard as a rock."

"Marine, are you going to introduce me to your date?" His CO was standing next to them. They jumped apart.

They'd been so absorbed in each other they hadn't noticed.

"Crap," she said out loud, before wincing. "Sorry, I mean. I didn't mean to make out with the Marine in his uniform. I know you guys are picky about that sort of thing. Please don't be angry with him. That was all my fault."

What was with her mouth? It just wouldn't stop today.

"This is my, uh, my girlfriend, Chelly," Matt said.

Girlfriend? She guessed she was, but it was the first time either of them had verbalized it. For some reason it felt a bit awkward. Perhaps because his boss was totally giving them the stare down.

"Chelly, this is Commander Gray."

She held out her hand. "It's very nice to meet you, sir. I've heard a lot about you."

He shook her hand. "Call me Brenton. Mari told me that you're also a designer."

They'd been talking about her? "Yes," she said uncertainly.

"We weren't gossiping," he said. "When the lieutenant didn't show up at our last get-together, I asked where he was. She said you weren't feeling well, and that he was looking after you."

"Yes," she said, feeling guilty for keeping Matt from the party. "I'm not used to the humidity or the heat down here. I guess it sort of got to me that day."

"I'm glad you're feeling better. And I hope you'll be at our Fourth of July event next weekend."

"We wouldn't miss it, sir," Matt said, probably because he'd failed to mention it to her. "I guess we'd better get inside."

He guided Chelly through the doors.

Why hadn't he told her about the event?

"I forgot," Matt said as they sat down at the long table where all of the wedding guests were seated. "I'm sorry. With all the excitement of the wedding and everything going on with the two houses, I just wasn't thinking about it."

"It's okay. Do you want me to go with you?"

He paused with his mouth open. "What? Why would you even think I wouldn't?"

She shrugged. "You hesitated when you were introducing me, like you weren't sure what to call me."

He leaned toward her. "I'm always worried about scaring you off," he said. "If I say the wrong thing or if I push you to do something that involves my friends or work, I just don't want to upset you. And you've been really busy with everything, and I didn't want to add to it."

So he was walking on eggshells around her. That was the last thing she wanted.

"I think of you as my girlfriend," he said softly. "I'm just not sure if you feel the same way."

Oh. "I do. Think of you as my boyfriend." She nudged his shoulder. "You're right, I'm not one who is really into labels. But this is definitely a thing between you and me. So if you want to introduce me as your girlfriend, that's cool. And your friends are fine. We had a great time when we went out with Brody and Mari. I'm more than happy to meet the rest of your work friends."

He gave her one of those megawatt smiles. "Okay, then."

"Okay, then."

MATT WASN'T SURE what to think about Chelly. Part of her seemed to be really into the wedding, but then she'd put up a wall. One he wasn't sure he could scale. They were in the hotel room and she was asleep beside him. They'd made love, but she didn't quite give herself over as fully as she had just the night before.

The whole thing with the CO was bizarre. They hadn't talked about their relationship; she never wanted to. And he wasn't a big one to discuss feelings, but the feelings between them were intense. He'd never been in love, but this might be it. The idea that she might walk away at any minute really did tie him up in knots sometimes.

"You're staring," she whispered.

He chuckled. "Sometimes I'm so struck by your beauty, I can't sleep."

She sighed and then smiled, her hand traveling to his cock, which was hard. It usually was whenever she was around. A condition he'd learned to live with over the last month.

"Are you sure it's not because of this," she said, rubbing up and down the length of him.

"Maybe."

"Twice should have been enough," she said, scooting closer.

"Never seems to be enough when it comes to you."

He loved it when she was like this, her defenses down. So open and innocent.

"I feel the same way. In fact, I was just dreaming about you."

"You were?" He wasn't sure it was possible, but his cock hardened even more.

"What was the dream about? What were we doing?"

She let go of him and after tossing the covers off their naked bodies, she backed into her pillows. "You were doing that thing with your mouth," she said, touching herself intimately. "And your two fingers were right here." She began to moan and he thought he might lose control right then.

Before she could say another word, he was on his knees between her legs, pleasuring her. Using one of the pillows, he put it under her hips so that he had a better angle. His tongue teasing her in the way she'd described.

Moaning louder, her hand landed on top of his head, the other on her breast playing with one of her nipples—not a sexier sight in the world. This, right here, between them—it was more than sex. She might not know it, but he did. She bucked against his mouth. His little wildcat.

Here the walls were down and she was all his. It was one of the reasons he was always hard for her. That and she was gorgeous, smart...

"Come for me." His words were soft, and she obeyed. Her muscles tightened and squeezed as her body shook. She cried out his name. Watching her come apart was a privilege, one he respected, one he wanted every day. He stroked her hair, whispered in her ear what she meant to him. Everything. That was an easy one. She'd calmed and he put on protection. Bringing her ankles up onto his shoulders, he pumped into her slowly.

So tight for him. Making love to her never got old. Her ankles locked around his neck.

"Yes," he drawled and he increased his pace. His thumb continued to rub that little nub of hers. She groaned and pressed her hips against him.

"Tell me what you need, babe."

Her eyes flashed open. "You. Just you."

Sweeter words had never been spoken. The way she looked at him... Heat seared through him, going straight to his heart.

This was *his* Chelly.

She reached for his hands, and he clasped hers tightly as he thrust into her. Their gazes fixed on one another. The connection between them palpable.

His Chelly was special.

"Matt!" she screamed and her body bowed. His climax followed, giving himself over to the sounds of her bliss and matching it with his own.

A few minutes later her head was on his shoulder

and she was splayed against his chest. This is how he slept best, with her across him. And him holding her like he would never let her go.

16

MATT PACED OUTSIDE the pool house door. Inside, Chelly was getting ready. "Babe, we're going to be late." He'd already been waiting an hour for her. Patient as he tried to be, he hated being late. But she just didn't seem to care.

It didn't help that he hadn't seen her much all week. On Monday an emergency training session had been called. He'd been in North Carolina working with some of the grunts there on evacuation techniques. He'd flown home the day before to find she was on a shopping expedition with Mari in Dallas.

Maybe it was wrong, but he'd been disappointed when she wasn't waiting for him. He'd missed her so much. Then she wasn't even there when he got home. Selfish, maybe, but she didn't seem to understand why he was upset.

In fact, she'd been so mad, she'd slept in the pool house for the first time in weeks the night before. He was determined to make it up to her. To make amends because the last thing he wanted was her out of his bed.

"Five more minutes," she said. The same thing she'd been saying for the last half hour. "Babe, you're beautiful with no makeup and naked. Everything else is icing on the cake."

Today she'd come home when he was in the shower and announced she was going to hurry to change.

When she opened the pool house door, all thoughts left his mind. She'd arranged her strawberry-blond curls up on her head, and she wore a fitted red dress that hit her midthigh. She'd done something with her eyes that made the color even deeper than they normally were.

"Okay. You're gorgeous. In fact, it's an I-want-to-ravish-you kind of gorgeous."

She laughed. "I wanted you to see what you were missing." Her eyebrow rose.

"Trust me, I know. And I'm sorry. Can we chalk it up to the fact that I hadn't slept in four days and I really missed you? Forgive me?"

She sighed. "I'll think about it. Maybe if you behave tonight, you'll get a treat."

He smiled and moved closer. "What kind of treat?" He nuzzled her ear, knowing she liked that.

"We'll see. I think you might have trouble with the behaving part."

Then she slipped on some red heels; was she ever going to be eye candy for the entire party.

"I'm not really sure I want to share you with anyone else tonight. I'm feeling more and more selfish."

She glanced back at him and grinned. "Come on,

Marine, you're the one griping about being late. Don't want to miss the fireworks."

"Babe, there could be fireworks right here."

"Like I said, behave yourself, and maybe you'll see those private fireworks later."

"I have to wait that long?"

She laughed all the way out to the truck.

Maybe they'd be okay, after all.

"You guys seem serious about each other," Carissa, the CO's niece, said. It almost sounded as if she was disappointed. She was a pretty girl, but talkative, and her questions had been a bit too personal for Chelly's taste.

The party was in full swing when she and Matt had arrived. Most of it happening out on the deck of the CO's place—a sprawling seaside house that took minimalism to a new height.

They'd been cornered by Carissa for the last ten minutes. She'd been peppering them with questions about their relationship, and Chelly was beginning to think she might work for the CIA or something. There seemed to be no aspect she wouldn't pounce on.

"Chelly and I are just having a good time together," Matt said. But it was how he said it that didn't sit quite right with Chelly. Why not say they were dating? Was it that big of a deal that they migh be attached? That was what she wanted, right?

Right. Or...

Don't be stupid. You're the one who runs when things get too serious. He's just trying to keep it light.

"Chelly's been great helping me with the house I'm

building and getting my parents' house in shape. I couldn't have done any of it without her. She's the most amazing woman I've ever met."

At least he'd said that. She should be happy. The projects were in good shape. She'd made some real friends. And she was with a great guy.

So why am I this sad?

The kind of sad that would normally have her running away from the party in tears. Except she couldn't do that because he hadn't done anything wrong. And this night was important to him. There was no way she'd ruin it for Matt.

Put your big girl panties on and get it together. This was really about the fact that she'd been angry at him for being annoyed with her about her trip to Dallas.

First of all, she had no idea when he'd be home. That was classified.

Second, Mari only had that one day when she could go to The Market in Dallas, which might be Chelly's new favorite place in the world. They'd found all the missing pieces she needed for both of his places. She'd tried to explain that to him, but he'd been so unreasonable. He'd never acted like that before and it reminded her of her ex.

Still, this party was about him, and she wouldn't do anything to cause Matt trouble. Besides, he'd been really sweet before they'd arrived here, and they'd both been tired that night when she'd finally made it home at midnight from her shopping trip.

"It helps to have a client who knows what he wants,"

she said, surprised by how cheerful her voice sounded. Maybe she could do this.

"Huh. So you guys *aren't* a couple?" Carissa wouldn't seem to let it go. What was wrong with this woman? Was she going to hit on Matt? Because Chelly could only be pushed so far before she caused bodily harm.

"Look, there's Brody and Mari," Chelly said abruptly. She gave Mari what she hoped was a beseeching look and the other woman waved them over. "We should go say hello." She grabbed Matt by the elbow and yanked him toward the other couple. They were standing out on the deck facing the ocean. It was blessedly cooler and she tried not to gulp the fresh air.

"I totally get what they say about the glow," Chelly said. "You are radiant tonight."

Mari fanned herself. "It's four days of a honeymoon with this guy," she said, pointing to Brody. "I've never been so pampered in my life. And a lot of that is thanks to you, Matt. If you hadn't been able to handle the training, we would have had to postpone our honeymoon, probably until I was too fat and miserable to enjoy it."

"No problem," Matt said. "Glad to see you guys had a good time."

Mari hooked her arm in Chelly's. "I'm borrowing my new favorite designer to talk shop. You boys keep yourselves entertained, but stay away from the man-eater," Mari ordered, and she waved a finger toward Carissa's back. Brody kissed her cheek and then gave her a wink.

"Man-eater?"

"It's a long story," Mari whispered as she led Chelly down the steps to the beach. "Lose your shoes," she said when they reached the lower platform. They walked for a bit on the sand.

"I saw the stricken look on your face. I mean, you covered it up fast, but I was watching you close. What's happened?" Mari prodded.

Chelly stopped and stared at the waves. "Nothing." They were friends, but Chelly didn't know what she should say. She was one of the few business contacts she'd made, and she was worried about crossing the line. And, technically, they were Matt's friends. She and Mari had chatted non-stop on the plane to Dallas and back, but it was about the various jobs they were working on.

And really, what was there to share? The guy she'd been living with referred to her as just a business associate he was having fun with. Didn't exactly put her in the best light. She was making too much of it. But they'd just had the boyfriend and girlfriend talk a week ago, and she didn't understand why he wouldn't say yes to the question: Are you a couple?

"It's how she is," Mari said. "Carissa's always got her nose in everyone's life. It doesn't necessarily mean she's hot for Matt. I think she just likes to gossip. Maybe she should have gone to journalism school because she's good at it."

"It was feeling a bit third degree-ish," Chelly said. "Almost to the point of rude."

The other woman laughed. "That's how she rolls. You know, if there's something wrong, you can talk to me. We're businesswomen, but I think of you as a friend. And I have a feeling we'll be hanging out more in the future."

If I stay in town. Putting down roots had seemed like a good idea, but lately, things with Matt had been off.

Maybe she should stick to her gypsy ways and find another town. Might be too difficult to be so near Matt once things ended between them. "I appreciate that, really. But I'm fine. Just not used to strangers asking about my love life."

"In other words, mind your own business, Mari."

She grinned and put a hand on Mari's arm. "No. Not at all. So…I heard you were taking on the CO's house. That had to be scary. Trying to please the boss and his niece. Was the minimalist idea hers or his?"

"And there's the switch to a different subject. It was a bit tricky at first. But Carissa's moving out, so I made the CO sit down and choose his favorite things using an old technique from one of my professors. I guided him a little because I'm not going to lie, he's your typical bachelor when it comes to design. But I think overall he's happy with the results."

"I like how you went with kind of a softer version of minimalism. It's clean but at the same time it feels like a place where you can relax."

"Thanks. The more I learn about the CO, the easier it is to understand him. Obviously. Still, you know what I mean. His work is hectic so when he gets home he wants the sea to be the view. Nothing obstructing it."

"Can't say I blame him," Chelly said, turning toward the water. "What about Carissa?" she asked.

"Oh, no. She's more a chic Paris salon kind of person. She mentioned she might want to use my company. Internally, I was screaming no, but she might be a good project for Abbott. That girl can go toe-to-toe with almost anyone. That reminds me, any word from Carrie?"

"No," she said. "But I'm not surprised. I mean if designers in New York and LA couldn't please her, how would my simple designs?"

Mari squeezed her arm. "You need to stop selling yourself short. There's not a darn thing wrong with your designs. I'd put them up against anyone else's in the world. You need to own the fact that you're untraditional and maybe a little wild, but that's your thing. It works for you."

"Untraditional. Is that another word for flaky?"

Mari smiled. "No. It means you think outside the box, which in design is a very good thing. A lot of the projects I do, and I own this, are kind of the same. People see my portfolio and they want the same sort of thing. I envy you working on projects like Matt's river house, where you're doing something so different. How's it coming along?"

"Good. Meanwhile, Matt's parents' house was supposed to be a simple job, but every time we tear something out, there's another problem. Matt's got no clue. He's been away. I've managed to keep it well below budget, though. Want to see the new kitchen?"

Mari nodded and Chelly pulled out her cell.

"Wow. That's marvelous. And you did it under budget?"

"Yes. It helped that the cabinets could stay. They were solid maple. Moving the window was the big problem. However, we did it. Or Cal did. Thank you again for sharing your contacts. He's been a lifesaver."

"He is. And he only hires the best people. I always think I'm busy, but I don't know how he keeps up with it all. But I can see why Matt's so impressed with you."

"Is he?" Chelly wasn't sure what to think anymore, especially after his comment to Carissa.

"Yes. How could he not be? You do terrific work, and I admire how you refurbish old things into new. I could have used you when I was redoing my house. And you know those little buckets with the flowers on your website? I need about twenty of those for different projects."

"That's a lot of minnow buckets. You may clean me out. But thanks. I found some old thirties magazine holders I'm about to redo. Should have them up on the site next week."

"I might start asking to see things before you put them up. I could use something like that on my Magnolia project. Are they iron? I want iron elements in the bathrooms."

"Yeah, they have that scrollwork like the old sewing machines." It felt good to talk about business.

"Perfect." They were quiet for a minute. "Chelly, I consider you a friend. You believe that, right?"

Chelly faced her. "Listen, Mari, if this is about a baby shower, I'm in. I love doing things like that."

Mari laughed. "No. No. Though I might take you up on that." Mari grabbed her hands and squeezed. "If you need a friend, a girlfriend to talk to about, you know, men, I'm here for you. I'm a good listener and I know how to keep things to myself."

Chelly teared up. "You are a sweetheart, and I do consider you a friend. I promise. To be honest, I don't really know what's going on with Matt. One minute I think he's really into me and the next..."

"He's definitely into you. He can't keep his eyes or his hands off you. I noticed that at the wedding reception."

She smiled. "But then with Carissa... You know what? You're right. He's been nothing but lovely to me. I'm just not great at relationships."

"I was the same until I met Brody. He's changed the way I think about love. I never thought I could care about another person so much. It's just weird. But I hope you find your weird, whether it's with Matt or someone else."

They hugged.

"Hey," Matt said, approaching them. Brody was walking next to him. "You guys done talking shop?"

"Never," Mari replied, chuckling. "I could talk to Chelly for hours. She's so talented."

"That she is," Matt said.

He could be so kind. Maybe she was reading too much into all of this. The CO was close to Carissa and maybe Matt didn't want him in his personal life. She understood that, although he'd already introduced her as his girlfriend to his boss. It had been the keeping things light between them tone that—

But wasn't that what she kept telling him?

"The fireworks are about to begin," Brody said. "You ladies want to watch them from down here?"

"Sure," Mari agreed.

Matt put an arm around Chelly's shoulders, and she almost pulled away. He must have felt her tense up. "Everything okay?"

What was wrong with her? She hadn't slept much the last few days. In fact, she hardly slept at all. She'd grown used to being beside him. But what if things were going south for them? The last week had felt strained.

That niggling feeling that maybe it was time to go beckoned in the back of her mind.

She glanced up at him. He was so good.

"Sure," she said. "Everything's fine."

But it wasn't.

She was saved by the first bursts of light flying into the air. For the next ten minutes they watched the fireworks. This should have been fun and romantic. But all she could think about was her future. She had some tough decisions to make.

And letting go of the Marine, before he decided he was tired of her, would be the hardest one yet.

MATT WASN'T SURE what had gone wrong, but Chelly was upset about something. Right after the fireworks she asked him to take her home. Saying she had a headache, she went straight to the pool house. He didn't want to bug her, but he was worried. All night she'd been acting standoffish. Maybe she really wasn't feeling well.

He'd planned to talk to her about what came next for them. The end was in sight for their projects. And he wasn't sure what they had between them, but he was sure he wasn't ready for it to end.

A phone rang, and he realized it wasn't his. Chelly's phone was on the kitchen counter. She'd left it there.

The number had a Nashville area code. Her ex? No. She'd said he was no good, and she was a smart woman. She wouldn't be talking to him. He remembered when she'd thrown her phone into the pool to keep the guy from tracking her.

More than anything, Matt wanted to answer to see what gender the voice was on the other end, but he let the call go to voice mail. That would be too much of an invasion of privacy.

Wrong. Just wrong.

He picked up the phone and headed out to the pool house.

He knocked.

"Matt?"

"I wasn't going to bother you, but your phone was ringing. I've brought it to you. Kind of late for someone to be calling." He shouldn't have said that last bit, but he couldn't help himself. "Uh, I thought it might be an emergency."

"Oh. Just a minute." He heard her shuffling around a bit. When she opened the door a crack, she held out her hand. "Thanks."

He gave her the phone. "Can I get you anything?"

She shook her head. "Nope. I'm good. Just need to rest. Thank you." But she wouldn't look him in the eyes. Something was definitely up.

"If you do need anything, let me know. I could go get you some soup or something."

She gave him a weak smile. "I'll be fine. See you tomorrow."

He'd seen that smile before. The one that she gave people when she was distracted by something else. Was she talking to her ex? Did they maybe—no. She wasn't like that. She put all her cards on the table. If she was moving on with someone else, she'd tell him first.

The very idea that she might be, though, tore at his gut.

Why hadn't he been more patient with her? What had he been thinking? As if she was always supposed to be waiting at home for him whenever he might show up?

That wasn't her scene. He even liked that about her. Oh, hell.

He was just like his dad. Didn't like change. Wouldn't let his mother fix up the house how she wanted to because he didn't want his daily routine disturbed.

Chelly had put so much effort into fixing up the garage apartment so he wouldn't have to deal with all the renovations.

Was he any better than his dad?

She'd done so much for him.

And then again, maybe this was her way of saying it was the end. That she was ready to move on.

He had no idea what to think anymore. One way or another, they had to talk about the future.

Soon.

17

THE NEXT MORNING Chelly woke to the sound of her phone ringing. Not again. But she checked and it was Cal. She had only slept about an hour because she'd received a call from Carrie's assistant. The singer liked the sketches, and she would let her know about a final decision in the next two days.

Chelly wasn't sure if she should be happy, or prepare herself for the fact that she still might not get the job. Nothing was a done deal until the client signed on the dotted line.

"What's up, Cal?" she asked, answering the call. "I thought you guys were at the river house today?" They only had to finish the flooring. Once that was done, the job was complete.

"We are and that's what I wanted to talk to you about. When I couldn't get you yesterday about the flooring, I tried Matt. He seemed really upset that this wasn't happening fast enough. I told him we were waiting on some final details from you. And he sort of... I just wanted to say I'm sorry if I caused you problems. I should have never said anything to him. But he's the client and he asked me directly, so I had to tell the truth."

Oh. She'd been holding off to see if she could get a better price on the bamboo from another dealer. "Cal, it's all right. But I told you I was waiting to hear back on the pricing."

"I realized that after I got your message. I did want to apologize again, though, in case there were any bad feelings."

She sighed. Frustrated with Matt for stepping in and telling off her tradesman when he didn't have all the facts."

Chelly didn't like to think in terms of last straws, but the past twenty-four hours, she'd kind of had it with his overbearing ways. Maybe this was the real Matt. Maybe the kindhearted sweetheart she cared so deeply about really was a controlling jerk.

She stomped upstairs to find him folding laundry. He looked so unassuming, so cute.

No. Don't get distracted. This was her work. Her professional reputation was at stake. There were boundaries. They had to start setting boundaries.

"Matt, why did you yell at Cal? I told you I had the project details covered." Chelly tried to keep her temper, but it was boiling over. The Marine always seemed to be butting into her business. It was his house, but she was in charge, and she didn't appreciate his undermining her authority.

If she wanted a future in Corpus, she had to earn the respect of those she'd be working with, and that was difficult with the fussy Marine commenting on things when he shouldn't.

He put the folded T-shirt on the coffee table and grabbed another. "What's the big deal? He said he couldn't find you, so I talked to him. Since I was the one who wanted the limestone floors in the kitchen, and the bamboo everywhere else, I don't see what the big deal is."

It was a dumb thing, but he just didn't get it.

"If I called one of your coworkers and said I needed a part for an Apache, and that if he didn't get it to me by seven tonight he'd be fired, how would that make you feel?"

He turned to her then and looked at her as if she was insane. "It's not the same thing. And the day I need someone to help me do my job is the day pigs fly B-52s. And I didn't threaten Cal. I just told him we had a deadline, and he needed to make sure it was met."

"But *I* need help?"

"Sometimes, yes. Things are a little disorganized, and I like knowing how all the pieces are coming together. Everything should always be in order."

Things are a little disorganized? To him, maybe her way of doing business was a little different. There were a lot of plates to keep spinning while working on two houses. But she had it under control.

That need of his to fix people, as if she wasn't quite right, reared its ugly head.

"It is the same thing, and that you can't see it… I'm done. I can't do this." She waved a hand between them. "It's not working. I'll finish the jobs because I refuse to walk away from my responsibilities. But as far as the rest of this is concerned, we're over."

"What are you talking about?" He stood and then moved toward her. "You're mad because I talked to Cal about something to do with my own house? My dream house."

Yes, his. Crap. This really was just for him. She had to make a break. It was more obvious to her now that things were not going to work with him. There was no way she'd be with a man who wasn't one hundred percent on team Chelly.

He moved closer, but she stepped back. "It's not like what we have is serious. Just sex. You've made that more than clear last night with your boss's niece. But it's complicating the job. From now on, this is strictly business. Apart from the job, we won't need to see each other. And until it's done, I think it's best to communicate through texts and email. I'll be moving out in the morning."

Then she turned and headed toward the stairs.

"Hey, Chelly. Stop. We need to talk about it. Where is all of this coming from? It isn't like you to be so—I mean…"

"What? Mean? Is that what you call me standing up for myself? Because that's all I'm doing. You're the one who's overstepped. You're right. It is your house, but up until recently you've trusted me to make it what you wanted. Has that changed?"

"No. Of course I trust you. I didn't think talking to Cal was a big deal. Like I said, I was just trying to help."

She faced him again. "No, there's a difference between helping and trying to fix something. Or someone. But here's a news flash, Mr. Marine—there's nothing wrong with me. I don't need saving, Matt. I never did. I've made it just fine on my own for years."

"That's not what I do. So you're saying me offering you the houses to work on meant I was trying to fix you? Did you forget that you were also helping me out?"

But he'd always been trying to jump in, and she was just too independent to accept that.

"You're right. I've helped you, probably more than you'll ever realize. But I can't be around a guy who wants to control me. You're nice, Matt. Really. But I don't think you can let go of this need to so tightly own your environment and everything around you. Life is messy sometimes.

"And for the record, I know where every single piece of the puzzle is when it comes to the job." She tapped the side of her temple. "I may not have pie charts or accounting sheets, but I can tell you we're twenty thousand under budget on the river house, and I just saved you another fifteen thousand on this house by finding some salvaged wood. That's why I couldn't contact Cal until later. I was busy finding replacement boards so we didn't have to redo the entire floor in the kitchen. And while I was at it, I found cheaper bamboo, much cheaper than the stuff you told Cal to go ahead and buy.

"Oh, and let's add in the fact that I've been selling your mother's furniture for you. We have exactly six pieces left, and so far I've netted you almost thirty thousand dollars. You do the math, Marine, and then tell me I'm not always on top of things. I don't need this from you. Whatever else has happened, I did trust you to be-lieve in me. You promised me that you did.

"But it was a lie. All of this is a lie."

"I—" He scrubbed his face with his hand. "You're overreacting. It was one phone call."

"If that was true, we wouldn't be having this conver-sation. And it's interesting. My ex said the same thing when I left him. Told me I was overreacting."

"Now that's wrong and you know it. He was abusive and frightened you. I'd never hurt you."

He was right. But she was too mad to let him have the point.

"No, just control me. Make me into your idea of what the perfect girlfriend might be. I won't ever live up to that ideal. And while I'm not sure you'll ever understand, you've already hurt me more than he ever could have."

"I just don't get you," he said.

"That's the one thing you are right about. You need to decide. Do you want me to find someone else to take over the jobs?"

"Absolutely not—"

"Okay, then. If you want me to continue, it's business only. I know how much you like lists. I'll make some up for you tonight. As I said before, if you have a ques-tion, please text or email. I would appreciate it if you'd let me finish this my way. So far we are under budget and we're making the timelines. We can continue to do so if you don't interfere."

She stalked off to the pool house and shut the door, locking it. He didn't follow. Didn't try to argue anymore. Why would he? It wasn't as if he saw what they had as anything more than a fling.

He was just mad that she'd called him out.

I'm the idiot who made what we had into something more. It wasn't his fault, but that didn't stop her heart from ripping into shreds with every breath. The part about him hurting her more than her ex ever could have wasn't wrong.

Tears threatened.

No crying.

She blew out a big breath. Yeah, ordering herself not to cry wasn't exactly working.

Dumb. Just dumb. She should have never slept with him. The tears flowed fast and hard.

When will I learn?

She needed a sign because she had no idea what to do next. She had to get out of there.

Her phone dinged and she picked it up. It was a text from Carrie's assistant.

You're in. But she wants you here like yesterday. I'm sending the jet for you. Will text deets in ten mins.

Her way out. Her sign. It couldn't have been clearer if the universe had tattooed it on her forehead.

Yep. It was time to go.

After blowing her nose, she forced herself to breathe. Then she started packing.

WHAT JUST HAPPENED?

He wanted to go after her and straighten this out. It

was obvious she had no idea how much he cared for her. It hadn't been about just sex since that first night. How could she not understand that? It was one phone call and he thought he'd been helping.

It was as if she wanted to pick a fight with him.

Then it hit him. Maybe she was needing an out. She didn't want to take what they had any further.

Things had been somewhat awkward since Brody and Mari's wedding, but he'd chalked it up to their being busy. Tired.

Just sex? No. She honestly thought that's how he felt? There was no doubt he needed to straighten that out. But he probably ought to give her some time to cool down so they could talk rationally.

A burning smell pulled Matt from his thoughts. The lasagna! He'd made Italian because he knew she liked it. He'd been hoping they could talk about the future.

He blew out a breath. That sure went great.

He turned the oven off and pulled the casserole dish from the oven. The cheese was a little brown, but it looked good.

Maybe he was controlling. It was just a part of his nature, but he'd tried with her. Why couldn't she just meet him halfway? One phone call about floors and she'd lost her temper?

Maybe she was right about keeping it just business.

You know that's not possible.

Yeah. He did.

He grabbed a beer and almost finished the can in one gulp.

Chelly was definitely upset about more than a phone

call. She'd been quiet since the party the night before. Insisting on sleeping in her bed. For the life of him, he couldn't figure out how to get her to say what was wrong.

Hadn't he told her that she meant more to him than anyone? Well, he hadn't actually said the words, but he'd showed her. Time and again. When they'd made love. He thought they had a real connection. Was he so out of it that he didn't know when something was real or not? He didn't make those connections easily, but he thought he had with her.

Then he remembered. The comment about him hurting her worse than her ex ever could. That meant she cared enough to be hurt.

Jumping up, he started for the door.

Hold it. Might be a good idea to go in with a bribe. There was a small framed painting in the study in the main house that she'd admired more than once. He'd give it to her. It wasn't enough, but maybe it would be a start. He ran to the house.

Sure enough he found the painting. It was one of his mom's favorites. And then he was running back through the house but skidded to a stop by the French doors. The sliding glass ones were gone, and it looked so much better. As he glanced around the kitchen, he took in all the new details she'd added. Her pops of color. He called them the Chelly touches. He toured the house as if seeing it for the first time.

It was a home. His stomach tightened as it hit him. His mom's vision—the sketches had come to life, and perhaps were even better in person. Chelly had kept the

idea of what his mom had wanted, and then made it…
more. A place anybody would want to call their own.

And she'd done the same out at the river house.

She was really good—at her job.

So that meant…

He'd messed up. Huge. How many times had she
told him about her parents always being disappointed
in her, because she refused to let them control her? And
the guys she'd dated before always finding fault with
her in some way.

But he didn't. He thought she was pretty close to
perfect.

In his heart, he had been trying to help, but it was
understandable why she didn't see it like that.

Yep. He'd messed up big time.

Outside, he noticed the lights were off in the pool
house. It was early for her to be asleep, but maybe she
was tired. Or she might be in the shower. He started
toward the building, but stopped.

No. He wouldn't rush her. She probably needed time
to rest. First, he'd write a note and ask for her forgive-
ness. She loved his notes.

Yes. Good plan.

An hour later, the painting propped on his coffee
table, he grabbed his letter and went to knock on her
door.

But she didn't answer. "Chelly, I have something for
you. And an apology. I get it now."

Still no answer.

"Did I mention I have something I'd like to give
you?"

Silence.

Normally, he'd respect her privacy, but he was worried.

He tried the door and it was unlocked. He stuck his head in. "Hey, I won't bother you if you're tired. But—"

No. The closet door was open and it was empty. "Chelly?"

After a quick search, he left the painting on one of the patio tables and checked the garage. Her truck was gone.

She was gone.

A muscle tugged in his chest.

That might have been his heart breaking.

"TELL ME EXACTLY what she said," Mari asked as she examined Chelly's painting. Matt had texted Brody, not knowing where else to go for advice. He was also hoping Mari might know where Chelly had gone. For almost an hour after realizing she'd left, he'd just stood there and stared at the empty space in the garage where her truck had leaked oil.

He'd tried to convince himself it was for the best. Wasn't like he was relationship material. And besides, she deserved better than him. That lasted a good five minutes before he knew living without her wasn't an option.

That's when he called for reinforcements. Well, texted for them. He was glad Brody had brought his wife.

He repeated his conversation with Chelly.

Mari frowned. "Something happened at the party. She was upset, but she didn't want to talk about it. Do you remember what you said when you were speaking to Carissa? What it was that first set her off? I saw her face. She looked stricken, like she was ill."

He shrugged. "We spent most of the evening hanging out with you guys. Carissa was asking a million questions."

Mari rolled her eyes. "Like what? Be specific. Did she hit on you? She's kinda known for that sort of thing."

"No. Not even when she asked if we were serious and I said we were having fun."

Mari's eyes widened.

Brody's eyebrows shot up.

"But we are having fun, or we were. Chelly and me. What's the big deal?"

"Please tell me you aren't that clueless?" Mari pointed an accusing finger at him. "Another woman, a beautiful one, asks you if you're serious about your date and you say it's only fun?"

He obviously was that clueless. "I don't understand."

Mari snarled at him, actually snarled.

"I got this," Brody said, quickly jumping in as his wife sat there shooting daggers at Matt.

He felt like he should take cover. He really had a way with women—a way of ticking them off.

"Matt, let me help you out here," Brody said. "When you're with a woman, one you care about, if someone asks if you're serious, you say yes. That she's the love of your life and you couldn't imagine your world without her. Especially if the person doing the asking is a man-eater like Carissa."

It took a few seconds. "Oh. *Oh.*"

"Exactly," Mari said. "And then you made her feel like you didn't respect her work ethic, either, so you hit her with a double whammy."

"But she's good at what she does. Look at this place."

She nodded. "Yes, but you trying to help isn't allowing her to do her job. If she asks for your help, like she did with the online storefront, that's one thing. But what you did with Cal, is quite another. She's trying to establish a career in this town. And she can't do that with you contradicting her."

"But I didn't mean to. It's impossible to understand how she organizes things. It all gets done and on time and under budget, but she—"

"Earth to Matt. You've just said she gets it all done and under budget. Why would you step on that? Simply because she does things differently doesn't mean she's wrong. You and Brody are organized to a fault, but we try hard not to make fun of your lists and your need to have everything clean at all times."

"That's not always true, this morning—" Brody stopped when she held up a hand.

"You're not helping, either," she said. "I didn't say we don't comment. I said we don't make fun of it or belittle you." She turned toward Matt. "You didn't purposefully set out to hurt her, but you have more power than you think. She's head over heels for you, and my guess is she's feeling as if you don't care about her in the same way. Like you don't think she's good enough for you."

"Well, that's about the dumbest thing anyone could ever say."

"Marine!" Brody jumped up. "Apologize!"

"What? Oh. Sorry, Mari. I didn't mean you were dumb. I meant, she's way too good for me. I wanted to tell her a million times how I felt about her. But whenever I tried, she got that look in her eyes, like she wanted to run. I never knew where I stood."

Mari chuckled. "Have a seat, husband," she ordered, "we're going to be here a while." Brody did what she'd said. No one messed with Mari.

Then she tapped her finger against her chin. "There might be hope for you yet, Marine," she told Matt. "So here is what we're going to do…"

18

CHELLY STOOD IN the middle of Carrie's recording studio and pursed her lips. Part of her still couldn't believe she was here in Nashville. Well, technically, she was about thirty miles outside Nashville, at the estate of one of country music's biggest stars.

Totally surreal. When she'd called Carrie's assistant to tell her she'd take the job, she'd been put straight through to the singer. Carrie had informed her that her private jet was en route to pick her up and that she'd be staying with her the next few weeks. Chelly hadn't had time to think. But she couldn't leave her stuff at Matt's, especially knowing the house might be up for sale at any moment.

Riddled with guilt for running, she did it just the same. She wasn't strong enough to say a proper goodbye. Not yet.

She'd made arrangements so that she could handle both jobs without missing a beat.

She wasn't even sure she was ever going back, except to pick up her truck, which she'd left at the private airplane hangar.

While flying somewhere over North Texas, her heart had seriously broken in half and she'd started to doubt her actions. Leaving probably wasn't the smartest thing to do, but she needed a break. Time to think about what happened.

She'd overreacted, of that she was certain. But while things had been good between her and Matt, there were control issues—or, not that exactly, but that she wasn't sure she could ever live up to his expectations of what he wanted her to be.

Maybe she wasn't the right woman for him.

"The equipment will be here in two weeks," Carrie said, drawing her attention. "We start recording in three. I know it's fast, and I'm asking for a lot. But can you do it?"

She gulped. That wasn't much time, but the space was only about eighteen hundred square feet, and a lot of that was taken up with sound boards and speakers.

"Yes," Chelly said. "But if we're moving that fast, you have to make decisions quickly and stick with them."

The singer laughed. "Bossy much?"

"Well, if you're hiring me to do a job, I want to do it right." She'd said almost those same words to Matt. That hadn't worked out so well. Not true. The projects were in fantastic shape.

It was just her heart that was an unmitigated mess.

"I hear ya. Sometimes I need a little reality check. And I trust you. You're the first designer I do trust. Any ideas so far?"

"Neon lights for sure. Do you have a slogan or some kind of motto you live by?"

Carrie held out her wrists. *Dream Big* was in a fancy scroll on one. And then *Be Bold* was on the other in the same script.

"That's cool," Chelly said. "And they would make a great sign."

"You're right," Carrie said, glancing from her wrists to the wall. "I love the idea that when I'm recording, I can look out and see that. I knew your designs would be a good fit. Just knew. My gut is always accurate, a hundred percent of the time, except when it comes to men. If you only knew, Chelly. I just can't get it right with the opposite sex."

And so, in front of the biggest star she'd ever met, Chelly sobbed. Loud. There was no mistaking what was going on. Tears streamed down her face.

"Oh, my. Girl, you got it bad. Who was he?" Carrie asked, her hands going to her hips.

Chelly shook her head. "Just the best man I've ever met. And I left. I just left him. And I'm here," she cried. "Sorry. I want to be here. I want the job. This is so unprofessional. I'm embarrassed." With no ready alternative, she had to use her sleeve to dry her eyes.

Carrie burst out laughing. Then she covered her mouth with her hand and immediately apologized. "I'm so sorry. I don't mean to laugh at your pain. But the sleeve thing reminded me of my little brother. He used to do that all the time and it drove our momma nuts. Let's get you some tissues, hon, and I've got a bottle of wine with your name on it. Heck, I've got one with my name on it, too. We can—what's that word when people are miserable together?"

"Commiserate?"

"Yeah," Carrie said. "We'll do that." She slipped an arm around her shoulder. "I've had a few broken hearts over the years, so I have a lot of experience with that sort of thing. But I've made a good livin' off that pain, so there's that."

"THEN THERE'S THE two divorces where the rats tried to take everything I own. And I'm only twenty-six. Don't be embarrassed about crying. I once fell to my knees in front of forty thousand people the night after the love of my life dumped me. I was singing a song we wrote together, and I just lost it. One of the worst nights of my life. Tabloids had a field day."

She was following Carrie through the long hallway back to the house. "Was that one of your husbands?"

"Oh, no. They were all replacements. Every man since then has been. But it took a long time for me to see it. But this isn't about me, it's about you. C'mon to the kitchen. I've got ice cream and pudding. I might even have some whipped cream. And if it's a really sad story, I might make you some of my Crock-Pot Heaven."

Chelly laughed. "What is Crock-Pot Heaven?"

"Girl, you have been missing out. Chocolate cake mix and pudding. You ever have lava cakes? It's like that. There have been times when I've eaten the whole thing in one sitting."

"Can't go wrong with chocolate cake and pudding," Chelly said, already feeling a little better. Carrie truly was a superstar and a lot more down-home than she'd been expecting.

"You are my kind of people. That's exactly what I say. You tell me your sad story, and I'll take care of you. Singing is about all I'm good at, but like I said, broken hearts are my specialty."

Maybe this was where she was supposed to be. Getting on that private jet wasn't such a bad idea, after all. "Thank you for being so kind."

Carrie turned and gave her a quick hug. "You know what, sometimes you just meet people and you know it happened for a reason. I felt that way when we met in Mari's office. I mean it about not being embarrassed. We'll get you sorted. That's what my momma used to say. She'd get so mad when I got worked up over a man. She always said there wasn't a man made who was worth cryin' over. She's been married to Daddy for thirty years, so I'm not sure what that says about their marriage."

They laughed.

"Come on now." She motioned to one of the twenty stools around the enormous bar. "Tell me everything."

So Chelly did. From the reason she left Nashville to what happened with the Marine.

"I hope you don't mind but I might start taking notes. This has got country song written all over it."

Chelly chuckled. "You can call it Wrong Turns."

The other woman nodded. "You might be on to something there. So this hot fella cooks, cleans and worships your body? Remind me again why you split?"

Chelly looked away. "Well, when you say it like that, I wonder, too. But he was always up in my business, wanting to take over. I never felt like I was good enough. I can't take that."

"I don't want to judge, but it sounds like maybe if you guys were a little better at communicating with each other, things might have been different. Did you ever tell him that you loved him?"

"Love? No. It's not love," she said vehemently.

Carrie waved a hand in the air. "Darlin', it so is. You can't have a busted heart, sob in the middle of my studio and think it's not love. You're a bright girl, you know the truth in your heart." She winked at her.

Love. Hmm, love. Nah. It couldn't be.

She was most definitely not in love with the Marine. Except...that she was.

Carrie was watching her closely. "Yep, Crock-Pot Heaven coming up. Don't you worry, hon. We'll figure this out."

Chelly sure hoped so because she'd made another wrong turn.

MATT WORE A path in the floor of the upstairs garage apartment as he paced back and forth. "What do you mean you don't know where she is?" He was about to lose it. "You're one of her few friends, Mari. If she was going somewhere, she would tell you."

"Whoa," Brody said. "Sit down and stop yelling at my wife before I have to bust your chops. She's pregnant. With. My. Child. Now calm down before I make you."

Matt ran a hand over his head. They couldn't find Chelly. She wasn't answering texts and he was worried about her. "Sorry, Mari."

Mari gave him a quick, knowing smile. She was talking on her phone. "What? When? Then that has to be where she is. That little stinker. No, it's okay. I'll call her in the morning. It's late. Thanks, Abbott."

He was about to come out of his skin, but it looked like she had news. "She's in Nashville—at least that's what Abbott thinks. Carrie's assistant asked Abbott to email over the contracts so she and Chelly could sign everything tonight. That has to be where she is."

Matt sat down hard on the sofa. How was he supposed to talk to her if she wasn't even in the state? Why had she run away? She'd done exactly what he thought she would. Still, it didn't give him the best feeling.

He figured she wouldn't take his calls since he'd texted her a half dozen times, with no answer.

"How'd she get there so fast? It's only been a few hours. And where's her truck?" he asked.

"Just a second," Mari said. She was reading something on her phone.

Then his dinged.

It was from Chelly. He shut his eyes and took a breath, never more wary of words in all his life.

Hey. Sorry I left the way I did. This job came up in Nashville. A good excuse at the right time and I took it. I was wrong. You were wrong. But I need time. I've got to figure some things out.

That was it.
Then his phone dinged again.

I saw your email. I appreciate that you believe in me. I think I have to do that for myself now. We've got your jobs covered. Everything will be exactly as you wanted it, and on time. Take care.

Take care?

Heck. That sounded like a *see ya later.*

"What does it say?" Brody was asking. "Is she all right?"

"She's fine," Matt said. His voice flat. "She is in Nashville. She's got the jobs covered." He kept staring at his phone.

"Something's wrong with him," Mari said. "I think he's cracked."

"Nope, he's processing," Brody said. "Wasn't long ago I was in the same situation. I've seen that look in my own mirror."

"What should we do?" Mari asked.

"Give him some space. I'll make sure everything's off so the house doesn't burn down around him."

"Good idea," she said.

"You know, I'm sitting right here," Matt told them. "I can hear every word."

"You're coherent. Well, there's that," Brody said.

"I feel like I should get on the first plane to Nashville and talk to her," he said. "I mean, I know she said she needed time, but I'm worried if I give her too much she...won't come back." That twisted his gut. "I told her in the email that it was my fault. Maybe she can't forgive me."

Mari put a hand on his shoulder. "It's sweet that you want to go after her, but don't."

"What?" Matt looked up to see she was frowning.

"She texted me, too. Give her the time she needs. Don't push too hard. I'm afraid if you do... I won't spoil her confidence. But she's aware she's just as much at fault. She told me that she has to sort herself out first. And that's all I'm saying. It isn't just you, Matt. It's been an intense six weeks for you guys. Maybe a little space isn't such a bad thing."

Except that he might die without her. Well, that was kind of dramatic, but it did feel like she'd left Corpus with a big chunk of his heart.

Time. Well, if that was what she wanted, he'd give it to her. Three weeks. But then he was going after her.

He typed back.

Three weeks. And then I'm coming after my heart, which you stole.

Maybe that sounded like a threat. It was. Chelly was his everything. He was going to make sure she knew.

She didn't reply.

19

GRIPPING HER ARMRESTS, Chelly held her breath as the plane landed. Always a nervous flyer, it didn't help that, except for the two pilots up front, she was the only one on the private jet. Not that it was a terrible hardship having to fly on a country star's private plane, but there was no one to distract her.

Admittedly, her thoughts about Matt were pretty distracting. She'd thought of nothing else but him.

That was one of the reasons she was here. It had been three weeks since she'd been in Nashville. Three weeks since she'd last seen him. Three weeks since her feelings had been crushed to a fine powder.

Now for a few hours she had to pretend to be one of the top new faces in design for a popular magazine. Matt's two projects had netted her a great deal of notice from the trades, and it didn't hurt that her biggest fan, said country star, was talking her up in the media.

Chelly had finished redoing the private music studio and an airstream for the star, and now she had more business than she could handle. So much so, she and Mari had joined forces. And her online business was bringing in more in a month than she'd made total the last five years.

It was hard for her to believe how fast her fortunes had changed.

A lot could happen in three weeks. That was why one part of her life was going so well, and the other part was a wasteland where her heart used to be. All she was capable of doing since the breakup was throw herself into the work.

Matt's projects were complete. She'd done what she'd promised, finishing them via texts, calls, a bit of Skyping and using go-betweens. Mari's assistant Abbott had checked on the job sites, using her phone to take videos of all the final details. His parents' house was on the market. He'd received an offer the first day, but the agent had suggested holding out a bit to see what other ones came in.

Matt had kept things professional, just as she'd asked. Never once had he tried to contact her.

She wished...

The only inclination to the contrary was that text he'd sent her the night she'd left telling her he was coming after his heart.

Now here she was in Texas for the photo shoot, and to decide on her next move. It wouldn't be to Nashville; it just didn't feel like home. Corpus did. But there was no way she could stay. Too many memories.

When the door of the plane opened, she jumped up

and grabbed her bags. "I'll help you down with those," one of the pilots said.

At the door, she was met by—Brody? "Hey," she said. "Nice surprise, but what are you doing? My truck is here. I can get where I'm going."

The Marine smiled. "Change of plans. Mari wanted to make sure you were delivered to the river house right away." He threw up his hands in surrender. "Before you ask, I have no idea. I'm just supposed to take you out there, and I do as I'm told."

She hoped there wasn't a problem with the job. From the photos Abbott had sent, everything had appeared to be great.

Brody helped her up into his big truck and put her bags in the cab.

"Strange that Mari didn't let me know before I left," Chelly said as Brody got behind the wheel.

"Probably happened while you were in the air. And hello? You've hit the big time, traveling around in private jets."

She laughed. "Uh-huh. Actually, they were bringing the jet back to get it fitted with something that's only made in Corpus. Despite everything that's happening, I've gotta keep a level head. Although the perks are kind of cool."

He nodded. "So is it good to be home?"

Yes and no. This place had felt like home once, but now she wasn't so sure. "It's good to see you. And I can't wait to see Mari. By the way, congrats, she told me you heard the baby's heartbeat for the first time."

Brody grinned. "One of the most exciting days of

my life. Well, except for when Mari and I got engaged and then married. That baby has no idea how much he or she is loved."

"Do you care if you have a boy or a girl?"

"Nope. Mari and I made that baby. I'll love the kid no matter what. I just can't wait. I mean, I know how hard it is. I used to have to take care of my step siblings, but what they say about it being different when it's yours is true. Nine months feels like a long time to wait, though, and I'm not a patient guy."

Sighing, she returned Brody's grin. Mari was a lucky, lucky woman. Brody would do anything for her, and there was no doubt how much he loved her and their child.

That's when she realized what she wanted most. What Brody and Mari had. That kind of love that left no doubts.

On the half-hour drive out of town she and Brody talked about all kinds of things, but she was grateful he never brought up Matt. Mari had probably threatened him if he did.

She had finally confided in her friend. Mari's advice was good about figuring out herself first. The same thing Carrie had told her. The singer had since become a great friend to Chelly. She'd been right about their being meant to know one another. They occasionally butted heads, but Chelly usually got her way about design issues. And while she'd never had a sister, it felt as if she had one in the recording artist.

When Brody pulled up to the house, Chelly's eyes watered. It was one of the most special places on earth.

Perfectly blending into the riverside, surrounded by trees, mountains, open sky.

Home. Only it wasn't hers. Pain tightened her chest, squeezing the breath out of her. It was all she could do not to tell Brody to take her back to the airport. This was too much. She thought she was ready to face Matt, and all of this, but she wasn't.

"I have instructions to take you out to the barn first," he said, but she barely heard him.

He continued the drive along the gravel road to the huge structure Matt had planned to use as his workshop. It would be filled with his stuff. What was Mari thinking?

Is she trying to hurt me?

Mari knew that Matt hadn't contacted her. In truth, she hadn't talked to him, either, other than asking about his choices for last-minute finishing touches. And Abbott had handled most of that.

Brody parked the truck and then went around to help her out, ever the gentleman. The Marines really did have a code.

The thought stopped her. Regret sat heavy on her chest. She shouldn't have run. If she'd been smart, she should have stayed and had it out with Matt. Told him what he'd done wrong and how he'd hurt her.

Carrie was right. Communication was key. They'd talked about everything, she and Matt, but not about what was most important.

And now it was probably too late.

"I'm gonna split. Mari said that I'm supposed to give you this." He handed her an envelope. "You're supposed to open it when you get inside, but not before. And don't ask me why she's being so cryptic. I have no idea. I'm merely the messenger and the driver. She's really mean at the moment, so I do everything she says. The doctor explained one more month and her moods should even out, but for now she's scarier than any enemy I've ever faced."

She couldn't help but smile. "She loves you so much."

"Oh, I know. And I love her as fiercely, but yesterday she threw a roll of paper towels at me because I said it was too early to think about baby names."

"Hmm. Yeah. You might want to go with the flow when it comes to all things baby related for a while. If it makes you feel any better, she told me that she felt like she was being too hard on you and she wasn't sure why you put up with her."

"Aw. Now see, that's why I love her. I gotta go." He pointed to the letter. "Open that, but only once you're inside the barn."

The day couldn't get any weirder.

"Okay. Thanks for the ride."

He gave her a quick hug. "See ya."

Brody pulled away and she stared up at the barn, curious about why Mari wanted her here. That's when she noticed there was a chimney. Who put a fireplace in a barn? That wasn't in the plan. And the basic structure had been up before she'd left.

She opened the door and expected a dirt floor. She gasped. There were bamboo floors, and the rough-hewn pine that made up the interior of the barn had been painted white. Near the fireplace, facing a bank of windows, was Matt's mother's desk from the pool house. The one Chelly had loved so much. As she glanced around, there were other pieces from the pool house. The daybed was angled in a corner with a bedside lamp and table. Another corner held a cozy chair and lamp for reading.

He'd turned the barn into a very girly office.

The perfect office—for her.

Wait. Was there someone else in his life? Already? Was that why he hadn't said anything?

No. He wouldn't do that. Matt was a good man. She understood that now.

Against the opposite wall were rows and rows of shelves. A lot of her inventory was displayed there.

Hold on.

Had Mari set this up for the photo shoot?

No one was that cruel. Mari knew everything about what had happened, and while she might be moody, she wouldn't do something so hurtful.

The envelope dropped to the ground, reminding her that it had been in her hand. She bent down and picked it up.

Mari better have a good excuse for this.

But when she opened the envelope, the letter wasn't from her friend. It was from Matt.

Dear Chelly,

Funny thing happened. Well, it's not really funny. You left for Nashville and took my heart with you. Probably because I didn't tell you how much I loved you. But I do. More than anything.

My life has been empty since you left. So much

so that this house—honestly, it's not what I want anymore. It isn't a home without you. I understand that now. I don't want to live any place where you aren't. You're home. You're my heart. I love you with everything that I am.

If there's a possibility you can forgive me, meet me at the boat dock. I love you with every bit of my being. I'll be waiting, Chel, for as long as it takes. But for the record, this has been the longest three weeks of my life.

—Matt

A sob escaped her lips and she threw a hand over her mouth. He loved her. So much so that he'd built this beautiful place for her.

She turned and took it all in. Everything she'd ever talked about with him when it came to her designs and what she'd want for her office was here. From the place to take a nap to the comfy chair to sketch in.

He'd listened and he'd remembered. All of it.

She had to force herself to breathe.

Matt loves me.

She'd asked him for time, and he'd given it to her. And all the while he'd done this. Created it without knowing if she would ever come back. He'd believed in her. Trusted her to know what was right.

I'm the fool, not him.

This was a dream. It didn't feel real. Her knees shook a bit, and her hands trembled. He was at the boat dock.

But she couldn't move. Was this happening? Maybe she was asleep on the plane and she needed to wake up.

She forced herself to take a step so she could glance out the window. The river was running rough, churning in much the same way as her nerves.

Taking a deep breath, she left the barn and followed the stone pathway down to the dock. Not sure how her shaky legs made the trip.

The pier was more elaborate than the last time she'd been here. There were flower garlands and twinkling lights draped around the steel posts and on the edge of the roof he'd added. She had tried to convince him that the fishing would be better during the hotter months if he provided a bit of shade. He'd done everything she'd mentioned and then some.

She followed the flowers and lights. At the end of the boat dock he stood there, dressed in his Marine uniform, holding a handful of wildflowers.

"I was worried you weren't coming," Matt said, his voice husky. He cleared his throat. He was probably as nervous as she was.

Why did I walk away from him? Dumbest move ever.

She held up the envelope. "I'm a slow reader." She sounded so calm, but inside not so much.

He smiled, but it was an anxious one, as if he was waiting for her to say something else.

She paused and took in the sight before her. From head to foot, he was glorious. Even now, the pull was there. That thing that connected them.

"It's okay, you don't have to come closer if you aren't comfortable. I promised to wait until you were ready and I meant it."

"I'm not sure I am."

"Oh." His shoulders sagged a little. "That's all right. It's probably a lot to take in." The expression on his face didn't change. He just stared at her as if he was taking pictures that would have to last a lifetime.

"I mean," she quickly said, realizing her words had been misconstrued. "Yes. It is a lot. And so unexpected. I thought we were doing a photo shoot."

He nodded. "About that. It's not really until tomorrow."

"What?" she said.

"The photo shoot isn't until tomorrow. I asked Mari to have you come in early so I could talk to you. I love you. That was hard for me to say before. It isn't now. Hard, that is. What's hard is living without you, not having you here is probably the worst thing I've ever been through, truly. I do love you. And if you'll let me, I'll spend the rest of my life making you understand how much."

"It's a lot." It was all she could say. Emotions overwhelmed her—happiness and dizziness, dang. She was so dizzy.

"Breathe, Chelly," he said softly. "I'm in no rush. I kind of put on the hard court press here. Maybe it was too much. But I wanted to show you that I care. What I couldn't do before. What I was afraid to do. I won't pressure you. Maybe—and this kills me to say this, but if you don't feel the same way—"

"I love it," she blurted out. "All of it. And you. Mainly you. So much."

He held out his arms and she rushed into them.

"I'm so sorry, babe," he said as he squeezed her tight. "So very much." He kissed the top of her head.

"I ran," she said. "I couldn't… I was a coward."

He chuckled and lifted her chin. "Nope, that would have been me. If it makes you feel any better, I knew within hours of you leaving that I'd made the worst mistake. So many times I almost flew to Nashville. But I wanted to give you time."

She gently slapped a hand against his chest. "You made me wait three weeks."

He dropped a light, sweet kiss on her lips. "I thought you were through with me. Not once in your text did it sound like you wanted anything to do with me. And then when Abbott took over, I assumed it meant we were over. And then I was afraid you'd think I was harassing you if I texted."

"Coward," she said, pointing to herself. "It hurt too much. Just seeing your name on my phone. So dumb. We hurt each other for no reason."

"Never again," he said. "If I mess up, you have to tell me. Don't run. And I will mess up. Even though I'm going to try my darndest not to, I'm not perfect."

"I don't want you to be. And I'm not, either," she said gazing up at him. "It's in my nature to run, but I won't from you. Never again. And we'll talk. But I'd rather you show me. I get it now. Those last few weeks, you were trying to show me how much you love me. But you were always worried that if you did or said too much, I'd back off. Your being bossy was you trying to take care of me. I should have been grateful."

He held her close and kissed her deeply. Then he

stopped and just held her as if he couldn't believe she was there. What little doubt she had was gone.

This was where she belonged. It didn't matter where they were; as long as she was in his arms, everything would be okay.

"I'm scared," she admitted.

"Me, too," he said. "But we'll do this together."

She nodded.

"One more thing," he began. "And it's okay if you want to wait, but I won't ever put off till tomorrow what I can do today."

What now? She smiled. "Okay?"

He bent down on one knee and then he handed her the flowers.

"What are you doing?" she gasped.

"I'm proposing, Chelly. Except for this river house, and probably a lot of frustration living with someone like me, I don't have a lot to offer you."

"That's so romantic," she whispered, beaming. Her heart was so full, it pounded in her chest.

"But I meant what I said earlier. I will spend the rest of my life showing you how much I love you. I want you to marry me. Today would be good. I realize that it's already been kind of a big day, so we can take some time. Maybe tomorrow. You can relax and then decide, though, no rushing or anything. It might actually kill me to wait to hear your answer. But I will."

"Yes. Whenever you want. I'll marry you, Marine."

"You're beautiful, Chel, and so smart."

She winked at him. "I know."

Then her Marine scooped her up and loved her hard.

MATT LAY THERE, looking at Chelly. They were in the bedroom of the river house. He brushed a hand along her shoulder. Just to touch her, to know that she was there.

"You're doing it again," she said, but then she smiled.

"Having trouble telling the difference between reality and dreams. I kept wishing you were in my bed. Every night when I tried to sleep and when I woke up in the morning—I didn't sleep as well without you on top of me."

She scooted until she was in position. "I had the same problem. My pillow was no substitute for you. I'm going to have to travel a lot for these jobs, but I have an idea. No more than seventy-two hours apart, unless you have some kind of assignment that takes you away for longer. I know you can't always control that. But with my stuff, I'm going to make it a rule."

He pushed the hair away from her cheek. "That's a great plan. But I get it if you need to be gone longer, too. You do what you must. I won't stand in the way of your dreams. Ever. My dad did that to an extent with my mom. He loved her, but I think he held her back in a way. He was pretty old school, and he didn't understand that he was hurting her spirit. I wish I'd understood that when they were still alive. Maybe I could have talked to him. Helped him figure it out like you did for me."

"Aw, Matt. You said they loved each other and I bet they did. You mentioned your mom quit the store because of him, but maybe she wanted to spend more time with him."

"Maybe. But if I get too bossy, or controlling, you

have to call me on it. Because I'm not always sure when I do it."

"Hey, sometimes I like it when you're bossy," she said, kissing his jawline. She giggled and stroked his shaft.

"And sometimes I like it when *you're* bossy," he said. "Like now. Tell me what you want, Chelly. You're in control."

She squeezed him. "Make love to me, Marine. *Now.*" She'd tried to make her voice sound gruff, but she was laughing.

Oh, yes, how he loved that sound. He loved every sound she made.

"Yes, ma'am." He switched their positions, caressing her body and nuzzling her neck just the way she liked. She smiled up at him.

"Matt?"

"Yes, ma'am."

"I love you," she said.

Yep. That was his favorite sound of all.

"I love you, too, Chelly."

"Oh, and Matt."

"Yes, love?"

"Can you do that thing with your tongue and your fingers? Like now?"

He chuckled.

"I live to serve."

* * * * *

Don't miss the next UNIFORMLY HOT!
romance from author Candace Havens.
Available November 2016
from Harlequin Blaze!

REQUEST YOUR FREE BOOKS!
2 FREE NOVELS PLUS 2 FREE GIFTS!

HARLEQUIN®

Blaze

red-hot reads!

YES! Please send me 2 FREE Harlequin® Blaze® novels and my 2 FREE gifts (gifts are worth about $10). After receiving them, if I don't wish to receive any more books, I can return the shipping statement marked "cancel." If I don't cancel, I will receive 4 brand-new novels every month and be billed just $4.74 per book in the U.S. or $5.21 per book in Canada. That's a savings of at least 14% off the cover price. It's quite a bargain. Shipping and handling is just 50¢ per book in the U.S. and 75¢ per book in Canada.* I understand that accepting the 2 free books and gifts places me under no obligation to buy anything. I can always return a shipment and cancel at any time. Even if I never buy another book, the two free books and gifts are mine to keep forever.

150/350 HDN GH2D

Name	(PLEASE PRINT)
Address	Apt. #
City	State/Prov.	Zip/Postal Code

Signature (if under 18, a parent or guardian must sign)

Mail to the **Reader Service:**
IN U.S.A.: P.O. Box 1867, Buffalo, NY 14240-1867
IN CANADA: P.O. Box 609, Fort Erie, Ontario L2A 5X3

Want to try two free books from another line?
Call 1-800-873-8635 or visit www.ReaderService.com.

* Terms and prices subject to change without notice. Prices do not include applicable taxes. Sales tax applicable in N.Y. Canadian residents will be charged applicable taxes. Offer not valid in Quebec. This offer is limited to one order per household. Not valid for current subscribers to Harlequin Blaze books. All orders subject to credit approval. Credit or debit balances in a customer's account(s) may be offset by any other outstanding balance owed by or to the customer. Please allow 4 to 6 weeks for delivery. Offer available while quantities last.

Your Privacy—The Reader Service is committed to protecting your privacy. Our Privacy Policy is available online at www.ReaderService.com or upon request from the Reader Service.

We make a portion of our mailing list available to reputable third parties that offer products we believe may interest you. If you prefer that we not exchange your name with third parties, or if you wish to clarify or modify your communication preferences, please visit us at www.ReaderService.com/consumerschoice or write to us at Reader Service Preference Service, P.O. Box 9062, Buffalo, NY 14240-9062. Include your complete name and address.

HB15

Sculptor Grady Magee wants one thing:
Sapphire Ferguson. She's sworn off artists, but how
can she resist a man who creates art out of scrap—and
one with cowboy swagger to boot?

Read on for a sneak preview of
COWBOY UNTAMED, the third story of 2016 in
Vicki Lewis Thompson's sexy cowboy saga
THUNDER MOUNTAIN BROTHERHOOD.

"Lady, you and I generate a lot of heat. You can head home to catch up on paperwork, but that's not going to change anything."

"Maybe not." She shoved her hands into her pockets and clutched her keys as a reminder that she was leaving. Just because he thought her surrender was inevitable didn't mean he was right. But she could feel that heat he was talking about melting her resistance. "I need to go." She started to turn away.

"Hang on for a second." He lightly touched her arm.

The contact sent fire through her veins. "What for?" She turned back to him and saw the intent before he spoke the words.

"A kiss."

"No, that would be—"

"Only fair. I've been imagining kissing you ever since I drove away three weeks ago. If you don't want to take it beyond that point, I'll abide by that decision." He smiled. "What's one little kiss?"

A mistake. "I guess that would be okay."

"Not a very romantic answer." He drew her into his arms and lowered his head. "But good enough."

The velvet caress of his mouth was every bit as spectacular as she'd imagined. If she stuck to her guns, this would never happen again, so it seemed criminal to waste a single second of kissing Grady Magee. She hugged him close as he worked his magic. She'd figured the man could kiss, but she hadn't known the half of it. He started slow, tormenting her with gentle touches that made her ache for more.

When he finally settled in, she opened to him greedily, desperately wanting the stroke of his tongue. Kissing him was exactly what she'd been trying to avoid, but when he cupped her bottom and drew her against the hard ridge of his cock, she forgot why she'd been so reluctant.

Wouldn't a woman have to be crazy to reject this man? Wrapped in his strong arms and teased with his hot kisses, she craved the pleasure he promised.

Taking his mouth from hers, he continued to knead her bottom with his strong fingers. "Still think we should nip this thing in the bud?"

Don't miss COWBOY UNTAMED
by Vicki Lewis Thompson, available in August 2016
wherever Harlequin® Blaze® books and ebooks are sold.

www.Harlequin.com

Reading Has Its Rewards

Earn **FREE BOOKS!**

Register at **Harlequin My Rewards** and submit your Harlequin purchases from wherever you shop to earn points for free books and other exclusive rewards.

Plus submit your purchases from now till May 30th for a chance to win a $500 Visa Card*.

Visit **HarlequinMyRewards.com** today

MYR16R1

7669

JUST CAN'T GET ENOUGH?

Join our social communities
and talk to us online.

You will have access to the latest
news on upcoming titles and special
promotions, but most importantly,
you can talk to other fans about your
favorite Harlequin reads.

Harlequin.com/Community

Facebook.com/HarlequinBooks

Twitter.com/HarlequinBooks

Pinterest.com/HarlequinBooks